E-115-1-18046   THU   7/98

7/10/98

DARK EMBERS
AT DAWN

DARK EMBERS AT DAWN

A Western Story

STEPHEN OVERHOLSER

Five Star
Unity, Maine

Five Star Western
Published in conjunction with Golden West Literary Agency.

August 1998

First Edition

Five Star Standard Print Western Series.

The text of this edition is unabridged.

Set in 11 pt. Plantin by Minnie B. Raven.

Printed in the United States on permanent paper.

Library of Congress Cataloging in Publication Data

Overholser, Stephen.
    Dark embers at dawn : a western story / by Stephen
Overholser.
       p.   cm. (Five Star standard print Western Series)
    ISBN 0-7862-1163-6 (hc : alk. paper)
    I. Title.
PS3565.V43D3   1998
 813´.54—dc21   98-22722

DARK EMBERS
AT DAWN

Chapter One

Distant thunder and a flash of lightning in the night sky made Cap McKenna think of rain, but, when he stepped out of his cabin, the red-orange glow on the horizon made him remember all of that dry grass out there. From this distance the prairie fire looked harmless, as pretty as a length of yarn on black velvet. Cap watched it, caught by the fascination of the sight, until a breeze hit his face. With that night wind came the smell of smoke and the sounds of stamping hoofs from his barn. Penned horses with the scent of fire in their nostrils were wild, crazed creatures bent on one purpose — escape.

Cap turned and hurried into his dirt-floored cabin. At his bunk he pulled on his trousers and boots. Shouldering into suspenders as he cleared the door, he jogged across the yard past the pole corral and through to the barn. With a glance to the east, he saw yellow-tipped flames sweeping across the broad expanse of plain. As dry as this season had been, that fire might jump Trapper Creek, and then he'd have trouble.

Cap was a man alone, and there was only one thing to do. He had to turn out the restless horses before they panicked, busting up the stalls — and themselves.

Throwing open the wide double doors, he moved swiftly down the darkened runway. By feel, he opened each stall. In the end stall he slipped a halter over the head of his saddle horse, a big, range-wise buckskin gelding. Freed, the other horses charged into the runway. Bucking and rearing in their fear and mighty confusion, twenty-four, wild-eyed critters wheeled, galloping for starlight as though wolves nipped at their heels.

Cap inhaled the hay and manure dust churned up by the hoofs, and coughed. He figured the horses would run from the fire and head for timber on the ridge half a mile behind his cabin. In the shelter of pines there they would mill around, bunching in the dark. By daybreak the plugs would be hungry and thirsty, and he could drive them back to the corral. So he hoped. But if the fire could not be stopped. . . .

The notion of losing his barn was one he did not want to ponder. The structure was new, built of squared, hand-hewn timbers and roofed with heavy pine shakes, a barn big enough and solid enough to last a man a lifetime.

Cap led his buckskin out of the barn past the corral and tied him behind the cabin. Even with the bitter odor of smoke thick in the air now, the saddle horse was peaceful and did not fight the lead rope. After a pat on the neck and a parting word, Cap grabbed his shovel and headed for the fire.

Trapper Creek reflected dim starlight like a silvery serpent in a bed of sand. Cap leaped over the creek and climbed the opposite bank. For the past three seasons he had homesteaded this land; he'd seen the creek dwindle to a small stream in the heat of midsummer. But this year it had almost dried up, gathering here and there in deep pools.

A thick cloud of smoke hit him. Coughing again, he turned his back to the fire. He dropped the shovel and retreated to the creek. Jumping down to the trickle of water, he yanked the bandanna handkerchief out of his hip pocket and plunged it in. Then he wrung it out and tied it around his neck. Pulling the wet fabric over his mouth, he climbed the bank, picked up his shovel, and began the battle.

Cap hacked away at weeds and tufts of buffalo grass and blue grama, and dug out deep-rooted sagebrush along the bank of the creek. When his bandanna dried out, he jumped down to the water's edge and submerged it again, then returned to the smoky fire.

He became aware of the breeze again. Night clouds swept overhead. Cap straightened from his work as the wind gusted around him. Enveloped in smoke, his eyes burned. The crackle of the flames grew louder.

Driven by the breeze, the fire charged out of the smoke like Jubal Early's army out of the fog. Cap backed away. He knew now one man with a shovel could not cut a line long enough or wide enough to turn this prairie fire away. If flames jumped the creek, they would burn all the way to his cabin and barn. Sure as hell.

Thunder boomed. The breeze abruptly stopped. In the eerie stillness of the storm's alchemy, smoke-filled air grew heavy. The last of the starlight disappeared as though a curtain had been drawn. He backed away from the fire glow moving toward him. Then droplets of cool water hit his face. Cap glanced skyward. Yanking the bandanna from his mouth and nose, he drew a deep breath. Instead of acrid smoke, a rain smell filled the air. Still the thunder rumbled like cannon fire. Suddenly the clouds loosed rain by the buckets. Cap turned his face skyward and let out a whoop. One minute the battle had been lost, and the next he stood drenched with a sooty bandanna around his neck, fat raindrops striking his beard-stubbled jaw.

A year ago Cap had greeted Mr. J. Stuart Reynolds himself when a high-wheeled buggy forded Trapper Creek. The splash of hoofs had brought him to the doorway of his cabin, and in the tufted seat of a buggy he had seen two gentlemen wearing long dusters and narrow-brimmed hats. They had been followed by a pair of armed horsemen, both holding new Winchester repeaters at the ready.

This strange sight had been made more so by the matched black stallions under rein. Cap had never seen a light vehicle pulled by ungelded horses. Reynolds had hauled back on the lines, halting his spirited team as he had introduced himself in a booming voice.

J. Stuart Reynolds. Cap had heard of him. Most folks had. The founder of the Reynolds Overland Transportation Company, he was an entrepreneur, a man who had gone bust somewhere back East and landed in Chicago with little more than an idea to his name. His idea had been to haul freight off the Union Pacific Railroad to Western settlements. As the story went, he had cajoled and borrowed, and had built his business. After the war the company name, Reynolds Overland, had become known throughout the West. The freight baron had grown wealthy, rich enough, folks said, to travel in the luxury of his own Pullman car on the U. P. line.

Cap had greeted the man as he had climbed out of the buggy, stiff-legged. At sixty-two, Reynolds had been prosperously stout with a trimmed silver beard reaching halfway down his chest. Pulling the hat off his head, he had slapped it against his leg. Then he had reached out and vigorously shaken Cap's hand.

"Magnificent view of mother nature in all her glory," he had said in a booming voice as he gestured downrange. "Magnificent!"

The second man had moved up behind Reynolds. He wore steel-rimmed spectacles. Fine featured with a small nose over a thin mustache, his gaze had darted back and forth when Reynolds introduced him — "Mister Stanley Ashworth, attorney-at-law."

Cap had shaken Ashworth's hand. A city man, he had judged, out of his element in wide open spaces. Cap had glanced past him. The two gunmen had held back, neither dismounting while their horses drank from Trapper Creek.

"What can I do for you gents?" Cap had asked. "Coffee pot's on the stove."

He rarely had visitors, certainly never any like this bunch. His homestead claim was tucked up close to the foothills of the Rocky Mountains, a good two miles from the wagon road between Denver and Cheyenne. That rutted road with a single strand of telegraph wire was all that connected the two frontier towns.

According to J. Stuart Reynolds, this was the logical place to change horses on the Denver-Cheyenne run. Fresh draft animals here would cut shipping time by half a day.

"Time is money," Reynolds had said, "and I'm here to offer you a contract."

Skeptical at first, Cap had listened with growing interest.

"Sir," Reynolds had said, "I am proposing a three-year agreement with a fee to you of one dollar per wagon, expenses covering hay and oats at Denver prices, horse liniment and medicines, and all the harness repair gear needed for the job." He had paused. "And a barn."

Cap had recognized opportunity when it hit him over the head. After discussing the dimensions of the barn, he had accepted the offer with a handshake.

The money had not been prominent in his thinking. His needs then were simple. True, he had needed the cash. Hard cash was necessary, if he was to buy breeding bulls and fill out his herd of cattle ahead of schedule. But the barn was what had done it. If he was to hang on here and carve a little ranch out of wilderness, then he needed a good, big barn.

Cap's end of the bargain was to tend company stock and provide meals and shelter for Reynolds teamsters as needed — about ten outfits a month, the exact number depending on the contracts from the Union Pacific Railroad in Cheyenne to markets in Denver. Reynolds aimed to run his six-horse outfits year around. Three tons of goods in every wagonload brought a tall profit at the end of the road.

Until that day Cap had been beholden to no man. Not by accident had he filed his claim in the wilds of Colorado Territory after mustering out of the Army. He had wanted solitude, and he had found it here. But lately he had caught himself muttering aloud. He talked to his horse more than necessary. To his credit, though, he had not yet demanded answers from the critter.

Over the next year Cap had come to know all of the Reynolds teamsters. Most were loud-voiced, shaggy men, accustomed to hollering at plodding, horned beasts and backing up commands with the pop of silk on the end of a bullwhip. A few were overbearing, profane enough to boil water in a bucket, but most were good-natured, modest men who welcomed a stopping-off place on a lonely road. Some of the teamsters favored two-handed poker to pass the hours while waiting out a storm, alternating card games with tall tales of their adventures with women. Others carried flasks and drank quietly, taciturn men who let a nod or shrug mix with "yup" and "nope" in what passed for conversation. A few were war veterans who craved talk. Sharing a pint of rye with them, Cap listened to their stories of battle between the blue and the gray, content to leave his own tale untold.

The teamsters proved to be a boon in other ways. On return trips they dropped off copies of *The Police Gazette, Harper's Illustrated Weekly, The Rocky Mountain News*, and all manner of food and goods from Denver or Cheyenne. No more did Cap have to saddle up before dawn to make the long ride into Denver for supplies. While he missed the excuse to tour saloons, drink his fill, lose a few dollars at blackjack, and take a woman to an upstairs room, he was willing to forgo those pleasures for now.

Cap logged the arrival of each Reynolds outfit. Every penciled X in his ledger book meant another dollar in his bank account in Denver. Reynolds had proven to be a man of his word. Not only had his crew built the barn as promised, to the inch, but he paid into Cap's account every month on time, in full.

But those damned plugs. Cap had not expected draft horses that were either half wild or three-quarters dead, and he spent more time chasing them or nursing them than he had bargained for. The plugs acted deaf and blind until a gate opened, and then they rushed it. They would as soon bite a man as plant a hoof in his skull, and Cap had to be on guard whether he was doctoring harness sores, lugging water to a trough, or slipping a feed bag over an ungrateful head.

At daybreak Cap saddled his buckskin. He swung up and set out after the runaway horses. Behind him the day dawned over several hundred acres of burned prairie. Wet and jet black now, the graze land was lost only to this season. It seemed impossible, but next spring the grass would grow back, thicker and greener than ever. He had witnessed this miracle. From the ashes of one season's fire came the lush green grass of the next.

He urged his gelding up the ridge toward a stand of tall ponderosas. Stumps and broken branches lined the slope where pines had been felled by the crew that had built his barn, and the earth was scarred in long vertical ruts where logs had been skidded down to the building site.

Halfway to the crest Cap reined up to let the horse blow. He took off his hat and wiped his brow.

The air was rich with pine scent as the sun warmed the

moisture from last night's rain. Needled boughs towered over-head, the branches swaying slightly against the brightening sky of morning.

Cap turned in the saddle. He gazed back the way he had come, seeing his cabin and barn in a field of green grass dotted by silver-gray sagebrush. Beyond Trapper Creek lay the black-ened prairie. Far to the east the horizon was a flat line dividing earth and sky.

Turning his gaze downrange, Cap looked at the foothills of the Rocky Mountains. He understood what Reynolds had meant upon first seeing this land. These panoramas stirred him, a vast and awesome view of nature untouched by the hand of man.

Cap rode higher. He had guessed right. On an open bench near the top of the ridge he glimpsed movement. The buckskin whinnied, tossing his head. Sure enough, when Cap cleared the stand of pines, he came upon the draft horses, all twenty-four looking at him as if to say: "What took you so danged long, cowboy?"

Circling the critters, Cap saw their heads swing around as they watched him. When he got behind them, he raised his hat and waved it, at once whistling shrilly. The horses stirred, slowly moving off the bench. They broke into a trot when pushed by the gelding — all but one. A bay mare plunged away, galloping from the herd. Hoofs tossing up clods of mud, she ran into the trees as though expecting to be shot. *One bunch quitter in every herd,* Cap thought, and wondered if that was a law of nature.

With a wave of his hat and a last whistle at the horses trotting down the ridge, he went after the bay. *Fool plug will be supper for a cougar,* he thought as his buckskin leaped ahead and took up the chase.

Cap tugged his hat down, bending low as the powerful

animal charged into the pine forest. Boughs slapped at him, showering him with water from last night's rain. The chase led upslope, angling over the rocky crest of the ridge.

Timber thinned on the other side. Cap raised up in the saddle and hauled back on the reins, slowing his mount. His cattle were scattered through the trees on this side of the ridge. This area was his tree claim, summer graze for his herd that offered ample grass and water as well as shade from the summer sun.

The chase ended here. The mare had halted at the fringe of fine, sweet grass growing along the bank of a small tributary to Trapper Creek. Cap rode slowly to the brook, ignored by the grazing bunch quitter.

But he was watched. The large brown eyes of horned cattle observed him warily through the trees. The animals had learned to avoid or outrun predators ranging through here, four-legged hunters from brown bears and grizzlies to wolves and cougars, staying alive by being nimble and always alert. In autumn, when Cap would ride up here to move them out of the timber, the critters would be half wild and all savvy, difficult for one man on horseback to chase down and drive to winter range at a lower altitude. A good horse and plenty of patience were needed to get the job done.

Cap urged the gelding to the bank of the gurgling creek. He bent down and plucked a willow branch. Guiding his horse closer to the bay, he raised the branch and swatted her across the rump. The horse wheeled and galloped away, heading back the way she had come.

Cap started after the critter, but then he heard a whimper. He hastily reined up. Turning in the saddle, he looked back.

At first he doubted he had heard anything at all, perhaps a water sound from the gurgling creek or maybe a jay in the trees. He listened. Under him, saddle leather creaked and the horse snorted and stomped as though disgusted at giving up the chase.

Cap heard nothing. He lifted the reins, ready to ride, when a second whimpering cry came to his ears. His head snapped around. Now his gaze searched the high grass lining the banks of the brook.

The cry came from somewhere in there. A chill ran up his back as he wondered if he had heard the cries of a bear cub. If so, the sow would be nearby, possibly circling him right now. In nature few wild critters were feared more than a sow with cubs.

But as he studied the grass and shadowed tree trunks, he realized cows would not be grazing here if a bear was nearby. The whimper came again, louder this time.

Cap yanked out his Spencer from the saddle scabbard and swung down. Rifle at the ready, he moved into the high grass, now hearing only gurgling water. He stepped gingerly through the grass, first looking downward, then left and right. Turning upstream, a brown shape caught his eye.

He stepped into the stream. He waded in shallow water where trout minnows darted away like slivered shadows. Then he recognized the dull color of an army blanket in the green grass a few paces ahead.

Reaching the bundle, he stepped out of the cold water. He knelt. Sure enough, this was a government issue blanket, neatly wrapped into a triangular bundle. The bundle moved. Cap lifted a corner of the blanket. He heard the cry again, a soft plaintive sound. One tiny hand reached out, the fingers flexing into a fist.

Disbelieving, Cap opened the blanket. He saw the face of an infant, round-cheeked with shiny dark eyes, skin the color of creamed coffee. The baby cried out, blinking against the light of a morning sky.

Chapter Two

Cap lifted the naked infant out of the blanket, watching the tiny fists waving and feet kicking. The thick hair on the baby's head was coal black and curly. He appeared well fed and healthy, eagerly sucking on Cap's little finger after he touched his soft chin. Then the baby cried in a small, persistent voice.

Obviously, no mother willingly abandons her newborn, Cap thought, wrapping the blanket around him. He looked in all directions, half expecting to see the mother lurking in the trees nearby. But the forest shadows were still.

Cap stood, holding the baby boy in the crook of one arm. The infant blinked, small dark eyes fixed on Cap's face.

"You're fat and sassy, now," he said aloud, "but you need Mama's milk, don't you?"

Cap waded the creek and walked through the high grass to his horse. He shoved the rifle into the saddle scabbard. Grabbing the horn with his free hand, he thrust a boot into the stirrup, hopped, and swung up. He took up the reins and rode into the trees with the baby cradled in his other arm.

He searched the immediate area for sign. Nothing. No pony tracks, no scrapes left by travois poles, nothing to signal travelers passing through. The forest was quiet. Cap glanced upward. No jays chattered in the trees. No furry-tailed squirrels leaped from limb to limb; no chipmunks bounded across the ground.

Cap had homesteaded here without any confrontations with Indians. On a few occasions he had spotted them from a distance, small bands of mounted Cheyennes or Arapahoes, or maybe Kiowas, all of them giving his cabin a wide berth.

He reined up suddenly. Bloody flesh had caught his eye. White bones and red meat lay on blood-soaked ground in a break in the trees. A corpse was there. The buckskin shied when the scent of blood hit him, and Cap reined the horse down.

He looped the reins around the saddle horn and drew his revolver, quietly urging the horse ahead. Now he saw that the carcass was not human. It was a steer. The animal had been slaughtered, carved, and skinned, a methodical butchering job that left no innards and little meat behind.

Cap holstered his gun. He had been warned that passing Indians would help themselves to his livestock, that savages had no respect for a white man's property or brand. Thievery was a mark of courage among them — so Cap had been told.

He was not resentful. A beef now and then was a small price to pay to the tribes who had roamed this land long before he got here. He rode around the carcass in a widening circle, searching the ground for hoof prints. The forest floor was covered with dried pine needles and old cones weathered to the color and shape of small beehives.

Finding no sign, he rode on. Then fifty yards away in a grassy meadow he spotted the prints of unshod hoofs. The way he read them, the riders were headed west, deeper into the mountains. He tried to follow the small imprints of two dozen ponies, but soon lost them.

The baby whimpered. He reined up.

Now what the hell am I going to do? Cap considered returning to the brook to leave the baby where he had found him. After all, if he had not come along, the baby would be in nature's hands. Either the mother would return, or a predator would discover the infant in the grass. If Cap put the baby back in that exact spot, wrapped just as he had found him, nature would take its course. . . .

A soft cry came from the bundled infant again, as though in response to Cap's dilemma.

Turning the buckskin, he rode back the way he had come and picked up the bay near the crest of the ridge. He herded the mare downslope. Coming out of the fringe of trees, he saw the Reynolds draft animals bunched around the corral and trough.

Cap had aided cows in birth. He had nurtured doggies until they could stand on their own. But when it came to the care and feeding of a baby, he was lost. Without help, this child would die.

He recalled having seen goats penned on a farm on the wagon road to Denver. Cow's milk would not be tolerated by a newborn, but goat's milk would sustain him. Cap knew that much from an incident in his own childhood. A neighboring family back in Pennsylvania had died of ptomaine poisoning from home-canned green beans, all seven members dying in their beds. An infant survived because she had been nursing. Cap's mother took her in until relatives arrived, and he remembered milking a goat for the crying baby.

Cap's head throbbed from the steady crying. Those cries stabbed at him. Time was running out. The immediate danger was from dehydration. He managed to get water into the baby's mouth a drop at a time from his fingertip. Then he used a clean cloth dipped in stove-heated water to wash urine and feces from the smooth skin.

After readying his horse, he fashioned a sling from a flannel shirt, and tied it over his chest. The baby fit snugly in it.

Cap left a note on his door for the next Reynolds teamster, as he often did when he was tending cattle, and rode out. The motion of the horse calmed the baby, and at last he stopped crying. Eyes closing, he slept.

The ride to the farm on the wagon road took half the day. Under a hot sun he saw the place. Amid yellow sunflowers, the low soddy was constructed of blocks of turf cut from the prairie. A footpath to the door was bordered by flowering hollyhocks.

Cap reined up in the yard. The flat roof was dirt, overgrown with tangled weeds, more sunflowers, and tufts of sun-browned grass. A ramshackle slab shed stood beyond the house, along with pens for pigs and goats, a chicken coop, and a corral for mules. On the other side was a battered Conestoga wagon, the spoked wheels buried deep in weeds. Cultivated land stretched out behind the place, a dozen or fifteen acres planted in wheat and corn.

Movement caught Cap's eye. A mangy black and brown dog trotted out from the patch of shade under the wagon. Baring teeth, the cur growled until the buckskin raised a hoof. Tail tucked, the dog slunk away.

"Hello, the house!"

Cap's call received no answer. After half a minute he repeated his greeting.

"Whaddye want, cowboy?"

The woman's voice startled both horse and rider. The buckskin shied, hopping sideways, and Cap struggled to control him one-handed.

Holding a tight rein, he turned and saw the woman peeking around the corner of the soddy — a single-barreled shotgun in her hands.

Cap introduced himself. "I've got a lost baby here, ma'am," he said, "and I need a little help."

"Baby!" the woman exclaimed. Lowering the shotgun, she stepped out from the house.

She wore a tattered ankle-length dress of heavy black fabric.

Hatless, her gray-streaked hair was pinned up behind her head in a bun, pulled away from her deeply lined face. Not old, Cap knew she was a homestead wife, her rugged life mapped in the contours of her face.

The infant whimpered. Cap saw the woman lean her shotgun against the wall of the soddy. She walked slowly toward him, head cocked.

"Well, iffen yer waiting for an invite, mister," she said, "get down offen that 'ere big horse."

Cap swung a leg over the saddle and dismounted. He stepped away from the buckskin and met the woman by the hollyhocks.

"Name's Missus Emily Haynes," she said, glancing at Cap before eyeing the sling. "Now, let's see that 'ere baby."

Cap shouldered out of the sling and opened it. He turned his upper body until the baby was shaded from the high, hot sun. Emily Haynes leaned forward.

"Oh, my goodness," she whispered. "Now, that's a wee one, ain't it? Few weeks old. Tar baby, ain't it?"

Cap looked at her questioningly.

"Nigra baby," Emily Haynes explained. "That's what you got, mister. Look at that 'ere kinky hair. And that's the skin of a darky. How'd you get a hold of it?"

Cap told her, and she interrupted him with a laugh.

"Jes' like Moses in the bulrushes, ain't it? Ain't it, now?" She smiled, showing missing teeth. "Well, what're ye gonna do with it?"

"I've seen she-goats in your pens, ma'am," Cap said, "and wondered if I could buy milk from you."

Emily drew back. "This here place might look like a prosperous farm, mister, but we got precious little. Got hungry mouths to feed, I do, sometimes with nothin' more than boiled wheat and jackrabbit stew . . . the stew iffen we's fortunate.

21

Some nights my boys go to sleep hungry. Their moaning hurts me deep, mister."

Cap nodded. "Reckon I'll head on to Denver, ma'am."

As he moved toward his buckskin, the baby cried. Cap heard Emily's voice. Without knowing what she had said, he looked back. Her expression had softened. She lifted a gnarled hand, beckoning.

"Oh, git in here. Git that baby outen the sun. Come on, now!"

Cap followed her through the door, stepping into one large room. It was as cool and dark as a root cellar. Plain and simply furnished, the interior of the soddy was partitioned by blankets suspended from the ceiling. After his eyes adjusted to the half light, he looked up and saw cheesecloth stretched across the ceiling. The fabric prevented dirt clods, débris, and insects from falling down.

Emily led him into the kitchen area near the back door. This part of the house was not partitioned. He saw a long plank table and two benches, and a black iron stove. The main room of the house was furnished with a platform rocker, four wicker chairs, a small table that held a thick Bible, and a kerosene lamp with a tall glass chimney.

Emily brought out a covered crock. She opened it and ladled creamy milk into a cup.

"Know how to feed a baby?" she asked.

Cap shook his head.

"Watch me," she said, taking the infant.

Cap looked on as she supported expertly the infant's head in the crook of her arm. With her free hand she dipped the end of a cotton cloth into the milk, and then let the baby suck it. She repeated the technique, smiling as the baby responded.

"Oh, you're the hungry one, ain't ye?" she said. "Yes, you are, yes, you are."

With a practiced hand Emily fed and burped him, and fed him again. She rocked him, cooing while he stared at her.

"Know how to diaper him?" she asked with a glance at Cap.

"No, ma'am."

"Better teach you," she said. "What goes in, comes out . . . sooner'n you might expect." She gently laid the infant on his back on the table, and retrieved a flour sack from a stack in the kitchen.

"First, fashion a triangle," she said, lifting the baby's heels, "and slide the diaper under his bottom. Then tie it at the corners, snug like so . . . not too tight." She looked at him and smiled. "Easy as pie. . . ."

At the clank and squawk of a pump handle outside she suddenly straightened, smile fading.

"Here, take him. Go on, take him!"

Cap awkwardly accepted the infant.

"See if he'll eat more." She hurried to the back door, adding over her shoulder: "That child's got to eat."

Cap sat down on the bench by the cup of creamy milk as Emily opened the door.

He raised the baby's head and tried to repeat the motions he had seen demonstrated. On his first try he dribbled milk down the baby's chin and chest. He wiped it off, and tried again. This time he found the eager target.

"Zeke!" Emily called out the back door. "Ezekiel, we got us some company, we do! Come in here and see!" She added: "Boys, git in here. Wash up first, now. Soon as you wash up, git in here!"

The farmer named Ezekiel Haynes ducked in through the door, his suntanned face, bushy brown beard, and muscular forearms still wet from rinsing off at the pump. Balding and heavy set, he was darkly tanned except for a marble-white forehead normally covered by his straw hat.

Four sons trailed after him. The youngest was first, face upturned and wide-eyed with anticipation. He was ten or twelve, Cap guessed as the others trooped in behind him. The oldest was almost a man himself with a patchy beard, perhaps seventeen or eighteen. Bushy haired with white foreheads and suntanned faces, all of them were stocky copies of their father.

Emily told them: "This here cowboy brung that 'ere tar baby." Her gaze swept past her sons to settle on her stone-faced husband. "Now, ain't that jes' like Moses in the bulrushes? Ain't it, Zeke? Ain't it fer a fact?"

Haynes approached the plank table, his thick legs in overalls swinging one after another like tree trunks. The man's arms hung loosely at his sides when he halted.

Cap was in the habit of standing to greet a man with a handshake, but with the baby in his arms and holding a milky cloth he could not easily get to his feet. He felt sheepish as he gazed up at the farmer towering over him.

Cap gave his name, adding that he homesteaded at the base of the foothills on Trapper Creek. "Reckon we're neighbors," Cap suggested with a grin.

Zeke Haynes did not smile or acknowledge Cap's greeting. "Mixed breed. Half savage, half nigra, likely." He looked at Cap. "Whatcha aim to do with it?"

Cap had no ready answer. "If I can locate the baby's mother. . . ."

"Mister," Haynes interrupted with a snort, "if the she-bitch wanted her baby, she wouldn't have dropped it into the weeds, now would she?"

Cap eyed him. "She wrapped him snug, as though figuring on coming back."

"Savages," Haynes said. "They ain't like you nor me."

Cap disliked this man. But he had to agree that a band of

Indians headed into the mountains to summer hunting grounds would be long gone by now.

"I thought some about taking him to Denver. . . ."

"Ain't nobody gonna take in no half-breed nigra to raise as their own," Haynes interrupted.

Cap held his tongue, knowing nothing would be gained by arguing with an opinionated man. He fed the baby while the big farmer and his wife and sons looked on.

"Reckon I kin tell you where the critter's father come from," Haynes said.

Cap looked up at him.

"Ninth Cavalry," he said knowingly.

"The Ninth?" Cap asked.

"Troop of bluecoat nigras," Haynes replied, running a hand through his beard. "Last spring a whole column rode through here. White officers leading black troops. Colonel's name was Sully. Said he had orders to keep the peace hereabouts."

The oldest son grinned at his brothers. "Sure enough looks like them soldiers made peace with the savages, don't it?"

Haynes shifted his feet and lashed out, backhanding the boy. "Git yer fool head outen the barn, hear? You hear me?"

The youth cast a fiery glance at his father, and nodded once.

Haynes turned to Cap. "I don't know where you stand on things, mister, but I can tell you mixing the races runs plumb against nature. Ye don't see sparrows mating up with robins, do ye? Dumb animals abide by God-given instincts. Man, he ain't got good sense. We're sinners, all of us, saved by Jesus, and we have to look to the word of God Almighty fer salvation. God commands us to be pure in His image, pure as His holy son, Jesus Christ."

"Amen," Emily said softly.

Cap noticed the boys avoided their father's severe gaze — all but the eldest. The patchy-bearded cheeks crimson now, he glowered at his father.

"Zeke," Emily said softly, "Mister McKenna, he wants to buy milk."

"That a fact," he said.

Emily nodded, warily eyeing him.

"The baby will starve, if I don't get some goat's milk in him," Cap said.

"Well, now," Haynes said, "most usually I'd say ever'thing I own is fer sale, Mister McKenna, at the right price. But I can't be no party to a violation of God's law. No, sir. We're Christian folk. We stand strong in our faith."

"Amen," Emily said again.

"Would ye be a Christian, God-fearing man, Mister McKenna?" Haynes demanded, bushy eyebrows arched.

Cap set the milky cloth on the table. Shifting the baby in his arms, he stood. "All I know is, Mister Haynes, this baby is innocent."

"The devil's messenger speaks in riddles," Haynes snapped, throwing his head back so that hair-filled nostrils seemed to flare.

Cap stepped away from the bench. Wrapping the baby in the makeshift sling, he turned to Emily Haynes. "Obliged, ma'am, for your help and advice. How much can I pay you for the milk?"

She shook her head, lowering her gaze.

Cap clapped his hat on his head. He walked through the main room and out the front door. Outside he blinked against the sun. He was hot — not from the weather, but from anger.

Cap secured the baby in the sling and swung up. With a glance back at the closed door, he rode away, heading south

26

for Denver. The baby fussed, but soon fell asleep with the motion of the horse.

Cap had ridden nearly a mile, when a shout reached him. Turning in the saddle, he saw a lone figure — a young man in baggy overalls running after him. From here the soddy was out of sight, hidden by a low hill.

Cap reined up. Pushing his hat higher on his head, he recognized the oldest Haynes boy. The youth carried a burlap sack as he ran awkwardly, his blunt-toed boots kicking up clouds of dust.

Breathing hard, he halted beside the horse. He took deep breaths and opened the sack. "Ma, she said fer me to give you these here items."

Cap looked in. He saw cotton flour sacks and four quart jars.

"Goat's milk?" he asked.

The youth nodded. He looked back.

"Pa, he's taking his nap. Gotta get home afore he misses me."

Cap dismounted. "What's your name?"

"Hezekiah," he said, turning to face him.

Cap took the sack from his big hands. "Hezekiah, you tell your ma thank you. She's a good woman."

"Yes, sir," the youth said. He started to leave, but then gestured admiringly to Cap's buckskin.

"Sure do like the looks of that 'ere cow horse," he said. "Trained for working stock, ain't he?"

Cap nodded.

"Someday I'd like to own a big, strong horse like him."

"Someday you probably will," Cap said.

The youth shook his head. "No, sir. Pa, he don't give me no money. Not one cent. I work hard, sunup to dark, but, when Pa sells our crops, all he gives me and my brothers is a stick of peppermint candy."

Cap said: "Maybe when he gets a little ahead. . . ."

"No, sir!" Hezekiah interrupted. "He won't give me nothing. He says I oughta feel blessed to have a roof over my head and food in my belly." His voice thickened. "I hate him, Mister McKenna. I hate my pa."

Cap watched him stare at his feet. Then he made eye contact again.

"Maybe someday I could work for you," Hezekiah said. "I'm a good hand. Don't mean to brag or nothing, but I'm a real good hand. I can learn the cattle business. Someday I'll prove up my own quarter section just like you're doing. That's my dream, owning a piece of ground." He added forcefully: "Mister McKenna, I'd do any chore you needed done."

"I run fifty, sixty head of cattle," Cap said. "It's a one-man operation."

Seeing disappointment in the youth's eyes, he added: "Tell you what, Hezekiah. In the autumn I generally have my hands full, moving cattle off summer graze and tending Reynolds' horses at the same time. Reckon I could use a hand."

Hezekiah's face brightened until Cap said: "Get your father's permission, and I'll give you work for a month or six weeks, come autumn."

The young man shook his head slowly. "Pa, he won't give me permission, Mister McKenna."

"Talk to him. Maybe he'll surprise you."

Hezekiah shook his head. "You don't know my pa."

Cap watched him turn, head bowed, and jog down the wagon road the way he had come.

Chapter Three

Cap rode slowly to avoid jarring the baby. In mid-afternoon the infant awoke with a cry. Wincing against a foul odor, Cap stopped to change the diaper. He tried to recall Emily Haynes's instructions for folding the cloth. Her hands had been nimble, her movements practiced and quick. And she'd had a table to work on.

Now, kneeling in the middle of the dusty, rutted road, Cap soiled his hands while fumbling with the dirty diaper. He put on the clean one and tied off the corners as best he could while the baby lay on the flannel shirt, crying hard.

"Moses," Cap said, picking him up. "Is that what I'm going to call you . . . Moses from the bulrushes?"

The baby stopped crying. Cap studied the little eyes fixed on him, thinking he had no right to name this child. He scooped up the baby, and they continued on their journey.

Nightfall caught him well short of Denver. He made camp in a clump of cottonwoods on the muddy bank of the Platte River. When the baby cried, Cap fed and changed him by starlight.

The diaper had leaked. Cap rinsed his flannel shirt in the river, along with the soiled flour sacks. He tried to wash the stench from his hands and clothes, but no amount of scrubbing with mud and sand removed it.

Next Cap tended his horse. Then he ate some jerky and opened a can of peaches from his saddlebags. After eating the fruit and drinking the juice from the can, he stretched out on the ground. With the baby in his arms, he fell asleep.

Cap was a man accustomed to laboring hard from dawn until dark. After supper he was usually busy splitting wood, hauling water to the trough, or mending harnesses by the light of a lantern. He was also accustomed to sleeping through the night after a long day's work. When the baby woke him, he blinked as his eyes adjusted to the darkness. Cap sat up, foggy brained and not knowing where he was for a moment. When his head cleared, he looked skyward for a clue to the hour. The black sky was filled with stars. He turned to the crying baby, knowing this was too danged early for man or beast to be awake.

By dim starlight, he again fed and changed the infant. Afterward he lay down with the baby warm at his side, slapping mosquitoes until he finally dozed off. At daybreak he was startled awake by the baby's cries. Even though groggy, he knew the routine he faced.

Afterward, Cap peeled off his clothes and stumbled to the riverbank. He waded in and found a neck-deep hole. The river had been named by French trappers — Platte for shallow. But here the water pooled. Submerged to his chin in the cool water, the current caressed him like a soft hand. He ducked under and came up blowing. From the riverbank came familiar cries.

"Moses!" he called, thrashing his way out of the river. "What am I going to do with you?"

Water glistened on Cap's lean body as he strode across a mud bank to his camp in the trees. He did not know what he was going to do with the baby, but he knew what had to be done now.

Cap dozed fitfully while the buckskin clip-clopped along the road. Head tipping forward, he jerked awake. His shirt under the sling was wet — again. The stench filled his nostrils — again.

"Damn," he whispered. "How can somebody so little raise such a big smell?"

Cap reined up, flinging the reins down as he dismounted. He was tired and hungry and short-tempered. Denver was still a long way off. He yearned to be there. He had dreamed of it — dreamed of soaking in the tub in the back room of Dave's barbershop, dreamed of cutting into a steak in the Rocky Mountain Café, dreamed of nursing a shot of Kentucky bourbon at the bar in the Denver House.

Wide awake now, Cap listened as the baby cried louder. He dreaded the set of tasks he had faced every three hours since leaving the Haynes farm yesterday. The stench assailed him, and he felt half sick.

Cap changed the baby and then peeled off his shirt. He was rinsing it with water from his canteen, when he heard a team and vehicle on the road. He lifted his gaze, seeing the dust billow into the sky — a freight outfit. Moments later he recognized the horses and heard the bellowing voice of a Reynolds teamster.

Dudley Dawkins was a small man with a shout able to rattle glassware, the voice booming from a mouth hidden by his drooping, tobacco-yellowed mustache. From the homestead on Trapper Creek Cap usually heard Dud's voice long before he saw the man.

Shouting or not, Dud was always recognizable. Without fail — hot or cold, rain or shine — he wore the same wide-brimmed hat of brown felt with a rattlesnake-skin hat band and the same dusty black vest over a red flannel shirt.

"Cap!" he shouted. "By damn! Cap, that you?"

Cap waved.

Drawing closer, Dud hauled back on the lines. "Whoa! Damn you, jugheads! Whoa!" He set the brake and jumped down from the wagon seat. Striding past his team of six, he asked: "What in hell you doing out here, Cap?"

The teamster drew up suddenly, planting his booted feet like a mule planting hoofs. "God damn! What stinks? Hey, that's a baby, ain't it? Hey, Cap, what in hell you doing with a baby?"

Before Cap could reply, Dud laughed. "Shit all over you, didn't he?"

"I was just chuckling about it myself."

"Hell, didn't aim to prod you, Cap," he said with a laugh. "But you gotta admit, you make some damned purty sight standing out here in the middle of the road, soaked down with baby shit and stinking all to high heaven."

"If you want more entertainment," Cap said, "watch me drive milking goats from Denver to my cabin."

"What in hell you gonna do that for?" Dud asked, turning his head to spit.

Cap told him about discovering the baby early in the morning after the grass fire, and his encounter with the Haynes family.

"So you're going into the goat-milking business," Dud said.

"Don't have much choice," Cap said. "I figure. . . ." Interrupted by the baby's cries, he knelt down and picked him up.

"Damned if you ain't got yourself a hatful of trouble," Dud commented. He paused. "Hell, man, let me think. Reckon I can give you a hand."

"How?" Cap asked.

"Rig's empty," he said, gesturing to the freight wagon. "I know a farmer outside Denver who raises goats. I'll go back and buy half a dozen and haul them to you. You pay my cost, and we'll call it square. The Reynolds wagonmaster up in Cheyenne don't need to know one of his outfits was used to haul livestock."

"Well, thanks," Cap began, interrupted again when the baby cried, more insistent this time.

"Yeah, Cap," Dud said, holding down a laugh as he backed away, "you got yourself a whole load of trouble there. A whole load of trouble, that's what you got."

Cap arrived at the cabin long after midnight, his head fogged by fatigue. He had dozed in the saddle, letting the buckskin follow the scent of water after leaving the wagon road. Trapper Creek guided the horse to the homestead.

Cap awoke when the animal forded the creek and climbed the bank. From the barn, a great black shadow loomed in the night, horses whinnied in their stalls. *Hungry and thirsty critters,* Cap thought, *needing attention.* Then the baby whimpered. He knew who came first.

Cap blinked against the bone-deep fatigue that dulled him. Never had he been so weary — not on the farm back home during harvest, not in the war, not ever.

He stepped out of the saddle, leaving the horse by the trough, and carried the baby into his cabin. One-handed he lit the lamp on a pine table near his sheet-iron stove, and unbuckled his gun belt. Hanging the holstered Colt on a peg, he moved to his bunk and put the baby down.

After changing the diaper, Cap fed him. By some instinct he did not know he possessed, he held him and rocked him for a time. The infant was lulled to sleep. Cap covered him and left him on the bunk. He blew out the lamp and eased out of the darkened cabin.

Hatless, head bowed, he started for the barn, mentally reviewing chores to be done before he could sleep. A whisper of movement came from behind. Too late he sensed or heard it. In the next instant a hot-breathed creature slammed into his back and clung to him with one thin forearm pressing

33

against his throat in a deadly grip.

Gagging, Cap was thrown forward by the momentum of his attacker. He staggered and caught his balance. Unable to breathe, he bent forward, struggling to throw off this critter squeezing shut his windpipe.

Cap felt a hard kick to his kidney. Consciousness slipping away, he sank to his knees. With more luck than skill, he rolled, driving a shoulder into the upper body of his attacker.

He heard a gust of escaping air and a pained sigh. The grip on his throat loosened. He inhaled with a gasp, nostrils filling with the pungent scents of buckskin and woodsmoke and sweat. He yanked the arm away from his throat and flung his attacker away. Gasping, he lunged to his feet and whirled to face him.

Or her. The figure, scrambling to stand, wore a shapeless dress of deerhide. Starshine gleamed on black hair tied into two long braids. On her feet now, she swiftly drew a thin-bladed skinning knife from a sheath on her belt.

Cap stepped back, eyeing the thin steel that glinted in the starlight. The woman crouched. In her shadowed face Cap saw large, dark eyes over high cheekbones.

Their gazes locked, they made a slow dance in the ranch yard. Cap turned while she circled him like a predator waiting for an opening. Alert as a cat for a moment of weakness, she was ready to lunge and plunge the blade into him.

Cap stretched his arms out, hands up and in front of him to ward her off. If he had to, he figured he could take one jab from her skinning knife, and then grab her before she could cut him a second time.

A whimpering cry from the baby in the cabin brought her suddenly out of the predator's crouch. She straightened abruptly, her attention drawn to the cabin door.

The instant her head turned, Cap rushed her. His hand

lashed out, and he grasped the thin wrist of her knife hand. He bent her arm back until she screamed.

He thrust a boot behind her foot and shoved. She stumbled back and fell, the knife blade reflecting starlight as it sailed end over end out of her grasp.

Grabbing a braid, Cap yanked her to her feet. He heard her breathing in ragged bursts and felt her taut body. The fight had not gone out of her. She kicked at him with a moccasined foot.

"Damn it all, be still. I don't aim to hurt you."

He doubted she understood, but, when the baby's cries grew louder, she ceased struggling. Her head turned to the cabin. Then she went limp.

Wary of her, Cap slowly relaxed his grip. The Indian woman did not move until he let go of her braid. Then she ran to the cabin, rushing through the darkened doorway. Moments later the infant stopped crying.

Cap strode to the cabin. Inside he lit the wick of his oil lamp. Replacing the chimney, he lifted the brass lamp and turned. Shadows leaped across the log walls. Then his eyes found and remained fixed on the young woman holding her baby. Seated on his bunk, she stroked the tiny face. She was young, maybe fourteen or fifteen.

Too young to be a mother, he thought. But there could be no doubt. The intimacy between infant and mother was unmistakable as she opened the front of her dress and nursed him. Her soft deerskin garment was simple and unadorned — and soiled where she had landed in the dirt moments ago.

Cap studied her in the light of warm, gold hues. Her black hair was parted in the middle. A braid tumbled forward when she turned toward him. Her gaze was straight on, a warning, and then she returned her attention to the baby.

Cheyenne or Arapaho — or Kiowa? Cap figured she be-

35

longed to one of the plains tribes that ranged through here with the seasons, but he did not know which.

"Can you talk my language?" he asked.

The young woman made no reply, not even raising her head to look at him.

Cap stepped closer. "Baby?" he said, gesturing to the nursing infant. "Baby?"

She ignored him.

"Well, I sure as hell can't say your words," he said aloud. Even so, he felt a need to convey his thoughts. He knelt by her side.

"You came back for your son, didn't you? I never aimed to steal him . . . just tried to keep him alive . . . keep him alive, until I figured out what to do."

Her reply was a stony glance in his direction.

Cap stood. He pulled the makings out of his shirt pocket. Having rolled a smoke, he lit the cigarette, using the lamp, and left the cabin.

Outside Cap smoked and gazed at a star-filled sky stretching over the prairie. Out of the vast silence night sounds reached him. A coyote yipped. Beyond Trapper Creek another chimed in with a long howl. Then he heard the hoots of an owl, a night hunter perched in a tree somewhere behind the cabin. Cap dropped the cigarette. He crushed it with the toe of his boot and headed for the barn.

He spent the night in the tack room, sleeping on the straw-covered bunk. He overslept and did not awaken until full sunlight. Hurriedly pulling on his boots, he strode to his cabin.

The door stood open. He leaned in and looked left and right. Empty. The Indian woman and her baby were gone.

Just as well, he thought.

After a breakfast of bacon and flapjacks and coffee, he stepped outside, buttoning a fresh shirt, his hat cocked back on his head. He tugged the brim until the hat was in place, and sized up a new day. He felt rested.

Movement drew his eye to the clump of aspens a hundred yards away from the cabin. Cap blinked. The Indian woman was there. She stood at the edge of the grove, silhouetted against the morning sky.

He watched as she faced east, the infant cradled in her arms. When she tilted her head upward, Cap saw her angular face bathed in morning light. She shifted the baby, lowered her head and pressed her lips to the small face. Then she stepped back, fading into the shade of white-barked aspens.

Cap did not move for a long moment. Last night she had been ready to fight or die for her child. Now he saw a young mother on the edge of the prairie, alone with her baby, and the sight stirred him.

Chapter Four

The clink of harness chains and a familiar shout brought Cap out of the barn. He had been cleaning stalls, and now he leaned his shovel against the door and stepped into the bright sunlight. Dud Dawkins was coming.

Cap was glad for the excuse to leave the barn. Mucking out stalls in the company of horseflies and mosquitoes was unpleasant, but the job had to be done to keep the Reynolds freight outfits rolling. Clean, dry floors in every stall was the first rule in maintaining good health of the horses. Accumulated wet manure and urine fermented and putrefied, leading to lameness, cracked hoofs, and crippling diseases like grease heel.

Cap took off his hat. He wiped his brow and moved to the pole corral while Dud forded the creek. Over the teamster's profane shouts Cap heard bleating, and sure enough, when the wagon drew near, he saw half a dozen milking goats in the wagon box, all of them down and bound to prevent them from leaping out.

Dud halted the team. Leaning forward, he squinted toward the aspen grove. "Who in hell's that, Cap . . . some Indian?" He stepped off the wheel hub to the ground.

Cap turned. The young Indian woman sat in the shade of the aspens now, watching them. From here the snow-white bark of the trees highlighted the pale green leaves like inlaid jewelry.

Cap relayed to Dawkins what had happened when he arrived home. Over the course of the day the young woman had not wandered far from the grove, avoiding the cabin until noontime, when Cap had set a plate of food by the door. Kneeling there, she had eaten quickly and then had returned to her baby in the aspens.

"Runs against an Indian's nature to be shut up in a log box," Dud said. He asked: "What tribe she from?"

Cap shrugged.

"Can't you palaver with her?" Dud asked.

Cap studied the teamster. "Can you?"

"Maybe," he replied. "A-fore I went to work for Mister J. Stuart Reynolds, I hauled goods for the Army. Camped with Arapahoes a few times. Fancy themselves traders, them Arapahoes do, and they palaver with sign when they run into a language they don't savvy. I do believe them Arapahoes could palaver with anyone in the world, if they put their minds to it. I picked up a little."

Dud spat and walked to the grove, raising his right hand in a universal gesture of peace. The woman stood up.

Cap watched them converse with words and hand gestures. Behind him, goats bleated unhappily from the wagon box. He saw the woman point south, sweeping her hand in the direction of the mountain range, and then she waved her fingers at Dud. She made gestures on her upper arms.

"Well, I don't rightly know what tribe she's from," Dud said when he came back to the corral, "but she was traveling with a band of Northern Cheyennes when she gave birth. The tribe was headed to a mountain valley for the warm season. She might be stolen from another tribe, I ain't certain. All I know is, she don't figure on going back. Cheyennes made her give up the baby. She broke free and came back for him."

Cap nodded. The account made sense, explaining why he had found the infant wrapped securely and hidden in the high grass. He told Dud what he had learned from the farmer,

Zeke Haynes, about the Ninth Cavalry.

"Oh, so that's what she was trying to tell me," Dud said, his eyebrows arching as he solved a mystery. "By damn."

"What?" Cap asked.

"She was signing something about buffalo soldiers . . . black troopers. She kept pointing to her arm and showing three fingers. Sergeant's stripes, huh? Must have been the Ninth she was talking about. And now she wants her baby to see the father. By damn, that's what she was trying to tell me."

Dud eyed Cap. "I seen the Ninth. Outfit's bivouacked near Denver."

Cap drew a deep breath and exhaled. He dragged a hand down his beard-stubbled jaw. The goats bleated again.

"Dud, I need your help."

"Hey now, hold on," Dud said, shaking his head. "Hold on one damned minute. I know what you're thinking. You want me to haul them stinking goats all the way back to Denver . . . and take that girl along so she can locate the father to her baby . . . ain't that it?"

Cap shook his head.

Dud spat and cocked an eyebrow.

"I'll take her to Denver," Cap said. "I need those goats hauled to the Haynes farm."

"The Haynes farm," Dud repeated. "What for?"

"To give to Missus Haynes as a thank you."

"That's a mighty handsome thank you," Dud said. "Milking goats, they don't come cheap. Dollar a head, that's what the critters cost."

"I'll pay for the goats . . . and your hauling time."

Dud stared at him, his heavy mustache lifting in a smile. "You're soft headed, Cap. That's what you are, soft headed." He added: "Hell, I can't take money from a feller who's lame in the brain."

His face awash in a wide grin, Dud turned and strode away. Over his shoulder, he hollered: "Stoke a fire and rustle me a bite of grub. I gotta roll, quick-like, if I'm a-gonna get to that farm and then all the way north to Cheyenne."

In the decade since its founding Denver had grown from a ramshackle mining camp of tents and shacks bunched at the confluence of the South Platte River and Cherry Creek, to a town of false-fronted frame stores, boarding houses, cafés, saloons, and dance halls. With a few sandstone buildings now, the newer structures were laid out in a grid of dusty, rutted streets. Surrounded by cabins and small farms, the town had taken on a look of permanence. And with a population swelling to five thousand, Denver sprouted enough chimneys to cast a pall of wood and coal smoke into the blue sky.

Cap saw that gray-brown haze on the horizon late in the second day of his ride. The sun in the western sky bore down on man and beast, as though a furnace door stood open, and sweat rimmed his hat and seeped through his shirt. This high plain with its pear cactus and clumps of sage and rabbitbrush was much hotter than the grasslands and timber of the homestead on Trapper Creek.

The journey had been painfully slow. The Indian woman rode a big plodding piebald horse, one of the few Reynolds draft animals broken to saddle. When they had started the trip, Cap had taken the lead, hoping the harness-scarred critter would feel inspired to keep up. Wishful thinking. Even when followed by a willow switch that Cap slapped across his rump, the plug held to a maddeningly slow pace. Nothing short of a load of buckshot in his south end would have hurried him along, Cap figured, and resigned himself to a long, hot ride.

He glanced back now. The woman rode twenty-five yards behind him, holding her baby in the flannel shirt sling Cap had given her. Her head and upper body were covered by the army-issue blanket.

It had been Dud who had convinced her to go. Cap did not know if she fully understood the reason for the journey, and all of yesterday and today she had been a silent companion, keeping her eyes downcast as she accepted food from him. She was unembarrassed when she opened her dress to nurse. She did not use diapers, but seemed to anticipate the baby's needs, and washed herself and her child whenever possible.

Cap drew rein at a log farm house on the outskirts of Denver. He was met in the yard by a stout, aproned woman who squinted at him, her hands planted on wide hips as he asked for the location of the cavalry encampment.

She stared at the Indian woman, face taut, until he repeated his question. Scowling, she pointed to the willows crowding the river. "Soldiers camped a couple miles down yonder, acrost the Platte."

Cap started to thank her, but she cut him off. "Mister, I'd get shut of that stinking squaw, I was you."

"Ma'am?"

"Folks in these parts got low regard for a white man taking up with squaws."

Cap eyed her. "When I need your advice, ma'am, I'll ask."

"Don't get sassy smart with me, mister!" she said, her face reddening. "Folks 'round these parts have buried friends and loved ones slaughtered by Cheyenne raiders. There's men hereabouts who shoot savages like you'd shoot a wolf or stomp a rattler. Go high-stepping into town with that savage she-bitch, and see what happens. Maybe then you'll remember a friendly caution."

She lifted her dress an inch, turned swiftly, and strode into the farm house, slamming the door shut behind her.

Cap glanced back. The Indian woman stared past him.

The wagon road paralleled the sandy bank of the South Platte River for two miles. Ahead, on the far side, Cap saw rows of canvas tents beyond a fringe of willows and cattails. He reined his buckskin off the road and splashed across the shallow water with the piebald following. Clearing the river, he crossed an expanse of dry sand to chest-high willows.

"Who goes?" came a sentry's shout.

"Name's McKenna," Cap answered, reining up.

A black trooper emerged from the thick growth of willows, bayoneted Spencer rifle at the ready. Although it was a hot afternoon, he wore a blue uniform of wool and a kepie on his head. His skin glistened.

"I have business with your commanding officer," Cap said.

"Ride through, sir," he said. He glanced behind Cap. "That savage, sir. She'll have to stay out."

Cap shifted his hips in the saddle, motioning for the woman to wait on the riverbank. She turned the piebald and rode back, stopping in the sand at the water's edge.

Cap rode through the willows up to the rows of small tents. He had not set foot in a field camp of cavalry since the day he had been mustered out in 1865, and now the sight and sounds of troopers at rest brought a swirl of memories to mind.

The rows of tents were straight, the grounds free of débris, and the weapons neatly stacked. *A clean and orderly camp,* he thought, *was a sign of well-disciplined soldiers*. Horses bearing the U S A brand were penned in rope corrals, saddles and gear nearby. Even though close to town, this was a field camp, not a garrison, and the troopers were required to be ready to mount and ride at a moment's notice.

Cap observed fire rings with coffee pots and mess kits in front of two-man tents. Some soldiers were inside their tents, flaps open, reclining on blankets. Others gathered in small groups, talking, smoking, occasionally laughing over a joke or exclaiming at the turn of a card. The large headquarters tent was marked by a guidon flying under the stars and stripes. This guidon was red, white, and blue with the number 9 in a yellow triangle. Nearby, six officers' tents were pitched in the shade of a stand of tall cottonwood trees.

Before he had taken the entire camp in, Cap was challenged by another sentry. He reined up and dismounted. The sentry took his reins, then Cap was led to the headquarters tent by a black corporal. The corporal asked his name, and ducked inside.

A moment later Cap was announced. Permission to enter was granted by a gravelly voice, and Cap ducked through the flap held open by the corporal.

"Mister McKenna, I'm Tom Sully. How may I be of service?"

Cap shook hands with the colonel who came to his feet behind a field desk. The man was stocky, thick-necked, bald as a cue ball with thin eyebrows over ice-blue eyes, and a trimmed mustache. Sully was in shirt sleeves, his yellow-striped blue trousers held by leather braces.

"Colonel . . . ," Cap began.

"Call me Tom," he said with a quick grin. "We're informal here. What do you go by?"

"Folks call me Cap. I'm homesteading a piece of ground on the Front Range north of here. Run a few cattle. Or they run me, often as not."

Tom Sully grinned again. He gestured to a folding chair by the desk. "Have a seat, Cap. Tell me what brings you here . . . a report of Indians?"

"One," he said, sitting down.

Sully looked at him questioningly. Cap recounted the

events since discovering the baby.

"And this savage claims one of my sergeants is the father?" the colonel asked.

Cap nodded.

"What name did she give you?"

"None," Cap replied. "I'd like to bring her into camp to see if she can identify. . . ."

"Sir, I'm afraid that's impossible," Tom Sully interrupted. His smile was gone, his jaw set. He spoke formally now: "We have regulations against savages wandering through our outposts, picking up anything they might wish to steal, or making outlandish claims against a soldier of the United States Army."

Cap hesitated before he spoke. "Then I'd like to speak privately to your sergeants."

"You have to understand, Mister McKenna," Sully said, "that it is, indeed, quite possible one of my men sired the child. I admonish them to steer clear of the savages, but these are strong, healthy men who crave the company of a woman, any woman. I issue orders and enforce regulations, but I can hardly lock these troopers in irons at night." Sully stopped, then added: "Obviously, the girl will claim a non-commissioned officer as the father. They're the highest paid enlisted men in my command."

"I'd like to give the father a chance to come forward."

Tom Sully stood. "Please understand, sir. It is difficult to hold these Negroes in my command out here on the frontier. I simply cannot allow distractions or any activities which could erode morale."

Cap knew he was being dismissed. Then he got to his feet and held out his hand.

"Thank you for hearing me out."

"A pleasure to make your acquaintance, Mister McKenna," Sully said, shaking his hand. "Sorry it could not have been

45

under more agreeable circumstances."

The colonel studied Cap for a moment as though another matter had come to his mind. But he said nothing further and stepped around the desk, escorting Cap out of the tent.

Outside, a trooper had already brought his horse around. Cap took the buckskin's reins. He thrust a boot in the stirrup and was reaching for the saddle horn, when he heard the colonel's voice behind him.

"Cap . . . Cap McKenna?"

He turned, seeing Sully standing before the H Q tent, his pale blue eyes fixed on him.

"Cap McKenna?" he said again.

"Sir?"

"By God, I just now put your first name with your last name. Did I hear right? Your name is Cap McKenna?"

Cap pulled his boot out of the stirrup and turned to face him. "Yes."

"I'll be damned," Tom Sully whispered. "By any chance . . . by any chance, are you the Cap McKenna who served with the Seventeenth Pennsylvania at Cedar Creek in 'Sixty-Four?"

"Yes, sir."

"Well, I'll be damned," he repeated. He drew a deep breath. "You don't remember me, I suppose, but I was adjutant to General Phil Sheridan the day he pulled you out of the ranks and made you a captain. You led the first counterattack against Early's Confederates, didn't you?"

Cap did not reply for a long moment. The company of soldiers here had stirred his memory. Now his mind flooded with images of Company B. Troopers in Sheridan's Cavalry Corps wore a distinctive white badge in the shape of a sunburst with a blue oval in the center and crossed sabers in gold. That patch was one of two items of war memorabilia Cap had saved. The second was a medal, a five-pointed star suspended from a red, white, and blue ribbon.

"I didn't know at the time it was a counterattack," Cap said. "I knew we got whipped that foggy morning, and had to regain lost ground or die. Some good men answered my call."

Tom Sully came forward, his eyes still fixed on him. "You're a modest man, McKenna. Phil Sheridan told me he'd win the war in thirty days with more men like you. You started the counterattack that turned the tide of battle. My God, man, the day was lost until you answered Sheridan's call and picked up the charge. Other companies followed you."

Cap well remembered Sheridan, the small, ungainly general on horseback bellowing orders while holding his saber aloft. The battle cry had been taken up when every man in blue that day saw "Little Phil" risk his neck to drive back the Rebs. Before it was over two horses had been shot out from under him, but nothing had stopped the man. Infantry and cavalry rallied, turning morning defeat to afternoon victory.

The captain and two lieutenants of Company B had been killed in the first minutes of the Confederate attack. After the battle, Sergeant Edwin Horatio McKenna had been awarded his rank by Sheridan. The men of Company B began calling him "Cap'n", an affectionate nickname, somehow shortened later to Cap.

"I confess I'm all the more regretful that I cannot grant your request, McKenna," Tom Sully said. "But perhaps you will be kind enough to grant mine."

"Sir?"

"Supper's coming shortly," he explained. "If you'll permit me, I'll have a place set for you. My officers will be honored to meet a genuine hero from the war . . . one who was awarded the Medal of Honor by President Lincoln himself."

Chapter Five

Served by black troopers in the officer's mess tent, the evening meal was the finest the Army had ever set before Edwin Horatio McKenna. Cap stared at the fresh vegetables and greens on his plate with steaming buffalo steak and potatoes and gravy. An orderly poured red wine into heavy pewter goblets.

He ate heartily and stared again when a dessert of lemon pie was brought into the tent, accompanied by brandy and coffee. Afterward, cigars and pipes were fired as the officers leaned back in field chairs, some loosening their belts a notch.

Cap enjoyed the meal, but, as a soldier who had been plucked out of the ranks in the heat of battle, he could not eat this food without thinking of the enlisted men, squatting around campfires, flame-scorched mess kits in hand. Their meal would be a ration of hardtack and three-fourths of a pound of salt pork. Aside from requisitioned food, that monotonous ration served with green coffee beans had been his camp fare for three years of his life.

In the field and on the march Cap had missed as many meals as he had eaten. During the war much of the food consumed by the men of his company had been scavenged from farms — pigs, chickens, turkeys, eggs, and root vegetables requisitioned by the United States Army. A farm boy himself, Cap doubted the farmers whose pens, barns, and cellars had been cleaned out by hungry bluecoats would ever feel much loyalty to the Union.

Colonel Tom Sully had introduced Cap to Major Luke

Symington and Lieutenants John Lowe and George Olson. The other officers of the regiment, he explained, were in the Denver House where featherbeds were a welcome respite from camp life.

"Gentlemen, seated at our table this evening is a man who shook the hand of Mister Lincoln," Sully announced, "after the President pinned the Medal of Honor on his uniform. Mister McKenna is a man of exceptional courage, a battlefield captain who led his company in the repulse of Confederate forces at Cedar Creek under the command of Jubal Early. Men like Mister McKenna led us to victory in that bloody conflagration that preserved our sacred Union and forever broke the chains of slavery."

Cap felt embarrassed by Sully's flowery praise in front of these young officers. It was true that he had shaken the President's hand. The ceremony had been held in the White House on a dreary, rain-soaked day a few weeks after the battle. Lincoln had grasped his hand and thanked him before moving on to the soldier standing to Cap's right. Cap would always remember the solemnity of the man and the deep fatigue in his cavernous eyes. Lincoln had not been an old man, but he had looked old. Barely a year later he was dead after the assassination that shocked the country.

The colonel delighted in recounting events of the battle at Cedar Creek. He described in rich detail the heroic ride of General Phil Sheridan. That battle marked the day, as Sully put it — "Old Jube got run clean of out of the war."

The conversation shifted to Sully's role as adjutant to Sheridan which had led to his present assignment. With wine sloshing from the goblet in his hand, the colonel became expansive, boasting that in accepting command of black troopers on the frontier he had signed up for duty no one else wanted. This hardship assignment, he said, would be rewarded by promotion to general officer and relocation to an established post back East.

"And then, gentlemen," Sully said, "while you are suffering summer heat and winter blizzards out here on the frontier, I shall have rejoined my wife and children, and once again be enjoying a civilized life."

The junior officers chuckled in a forced way as though they had heard the remark many times before. Conversation waned, and, one by one, the officers stood and filed by Cap. Each one shook his hand before retiring.

"A pleasure to make your acquaintance, Mister McKenna," Major Luke Symington said, coming last. "I was not inclined to believe Tom's tales until I met you."

Cap grinned and shook his hand. The major was a lanky man with light brown hair, clean-shaven, and eyes glistening with humor.

Cap took his cigar outside. Soon afterward an orderly brought his horse. In the gathering darkness, he was joined by Tom Sully who came from the mess tent. The colonel handed him a package wrapped in heavy paper — a warm bundle.

"Leftovers," he said, "to tide you over on the long ride back to your homestead."

Swaying slightly, the colonel added: "Wish I could help you solve the problem that brought you here. I truly do. But I follow orders to the letter, and require the men under me to do likewise. You've commanded troops, Mister McKenna. You understand."

Cap nodded. In truth he did, but not the way Tom Sully meant. During peace time, the Army lived by rigid regulations, endless drills, spit and polish. In war, regulations were buried with the soldiers who lacked the common sense to duck. Expediency became the rule. In Cap's experience, battles were won or lost by spontaneous decisions made amid the roar of guns and the screams of wounded men.

The orderly brought his horse. Cap took a last pull on the cigar, dropped it, and crushed the red coal under the toe of his boot. Shaking hands with Colonel Sully, he thanked him for the meal and swung up.

Cap rode away from the tents, many now glowing with candlelight. From one he heard a man singing "The Battle Hymn of The Republic" in a low, mournful voice. From another tent a banjo was softly strummed. With the musical sounds drifting around him, Cap guided his horse through the willows. He passed a sentry and rode across the sandy bank. Ahead water reflected starlight like a river of mercury. Crickets made their own music, quieting as Cap rode by.

As he neared the Platte, he saw a dark shape. Drawing closer, he recognized the piebald horse. The Indian woman squatted nearby, wrapped in the blanket. She stood when he approached. The baby whimpered. Cap gestured for her to ride downstream with him, where he would make camp for the night.

She did not understand. She backed away. Cap leaned down and picked up the reins of the piebald. He led the horse downriver. A swift glance back, assured him the woman was following. Five hundred yards away the arching branches of tall cottonwood trees made a canopy over the dry sand. Here, Cap halted and swung down.

First, he tended to the horses, then he gathered sticks and built a fire. He gave the package from Colonel Sully to the Indian woman. She cautiously opened the paper, smelled the contents, and then ate hungrily.

Night had fallen. In the dark sky Cap heard a beating of wings like urgent whispers. Moments later an owl hooted, a night hunter in search of mice. In the distance coyotes howled. Then from the encampment Cap heard a bugler blow taps, the long notes rolling through the darkness like old memories.

51

Another owl hooted and took flight. The soldiers were bedded, but winged hunters were out now.

Cap stoked the fire. Pulling off his boots, he lay back and rested his head on his saddle. He was weary from the long ride and, after the wine and brandy tonight, the crackle of burning sticks and the murmur of flowing water lulled him to sleep. In quick dreams the faces of the dead came to him — youthful faces of soldiers who had fought beside him, young men he had known well, young men who had died suddenly or slowly on battlefields already strewn with the bloating corpses of soldiers and horses.

Odd it was, that in his lifetime Cap's closest friends had been the men of Company B, yet, after mustering out, he had never seen any of the survivors again. Not one. Colonel Tom Sully was the nearest he had come to renewing an old acquaintance in the years since the war.

The visitor would have caught him by surprise, if the Indian woman had not stood suddenly, knocking over a canteen. Cap awakened with a start. He saw the woman edging away from the firelight, the baby clutched to her breast.

Cap sat up. He grabbed his Spencer, swinging the barrel around as he cocked the weapon. A deep voice came out of the darkness, faceless beyond the light of the campfire.

"No need to be shooting at me. I'm peaceable."

A big man emerged from the night shadows. He was broad-shouldered and all of six and a half feet tall, Cap judged. Unarmed and barefooted, he wore an undershirt and cavalry trousers held up by suspenders.

Cap lowered his gun as the black trooper came to the fire and knelt. Red-orange light from the flames played over his face — blunt nose, square jaw, and thick lips. His attention was on the woman who stood close to the horses hobbled at the edge of wavering firelight.

"Name's Joshua, Mister McKenna," he said, turning to Cap. "Joshua Potter." He held his hand out to shake.

"You know me?" Cap asked, grasping the big hand.

Potter nodded. "Suh, ever' man in camp's heard about you by now. A hero in the war, they say. You turned the tide of battle, they say."

"Don't believe those West Pointers," Cap said. "All the heroes are dead."

"Yes, suh, Mister McKenna. Yes, suh."

"Call me Cap," he said. "What brings you here?"

"White Moon Woman."

"Who?" Cap asked.

Potter pointed to the woman in the shadows. "White Moon Woman. Word got around about her, too."

"You know her?" Cap asked, surprised.

"Reckon I fathered her baby."

Cap stared at him.

"I'd like to see the newborn."

Cap turned and beckoned to her. The Indian woman stepped out of the shadows, her eyes on the big man.

Cap watched Potter stand. He faced her in silence. The blanket slid away from White Moon Woman's shoulders when she held the baby out to him.

"Oh, my," Potter whispered. "I have a son. My, oh, my."

He took the infant in his large hands and brought him close to his chest, looking at him by firelight. He whispered again. The baby began to cry.

"Looks like he's a-wantin' his mama," Potter said, grinning. He handed the baby back to White Moon Woman, watching mother and son for a time. Then he knelt by the campfire, his eyes on the flames.

Cap studied Potter as he lifted a burning stick from the embers. Potter held it up, and then let it fall back into the glowing embers. When he looked across the fire, he answered Cap's unspoken questions.

"White Moon Woman was traveling with a band of Kiowas, when we caught up with them last season. Kiowas was warring with Cheyennes. They done stole her along with a dozen other women and young 'uns after a raid. That's what our scouts told us. The Kiowas, they'd had a tough winter. Half starved, some was. Our scouts palavered with them. Said the slaves would starve first. So we gathered up women and children. Sent that band of Kiowas packing. Took us near a month to locate a tribe of Cheyennes to take the women and young 'uns." He smiled at Cap. "Kinda liked the notion of freeing slaves, I did." Potter paused. "White Moon Woman was willing, Mister McKenna. Get my meaning?"

Cap nodded.

"I never forced myself on her. Never. When she got back with her people, I figured we wouldn't see each other again. But I didn't forget. Many's the evening I thought about her. . . ."

Firewood popped, sending up a brief shower of tiny red flares. Potter's voice trailed off, and he gazed into the embers as though watching memories.

"You're certain you fathered the child?" Cap asked.

Potter nodded. "I was the only bluecoat with her. She stuck close to me. . . ."

"Sergeant Potter, attention!"

Cap was startled by the voice booming out of the darkness behind him. Joshua Potter scrambled to his feet and stood erect.

Colonel Tom Sully, in full uniform, came out of the night to the fireside. He was followed by Major Symington and two orderlies.

"Sergeant!" Sully said.

"Suh!"

54

"Sergeant, am I correct in stating you missed roll call twice this month?"

"Yes, suh," Potter replied. "The first time, mah horse busted loose. . . ."

"Sergeant, no excuses," Sully broke in. "Yes or no answers."

"Yes, suh," he said.

"Am I correct in stating you quit your tent after taps this evening?" Sully demanded.

"Yes, suh," he replied softly.

Sully stepped back, gesturing to Symington. "Major, put him in irons."

Cap stood when he heard the major utter the terse command.

The two orderlies came forward, both a foot shorter than Sergeant Potter. They hesitated, then grasped his arms, and led him away with Major Symington following.

Sully moved close to Cap. "So, McKenna, you found your man, after all."

"He found me," Cap said.

Sully glowered at him. "Convenient."

"Sir?"

"Fact of the matter is, you drew your man out."

For a moment Cap was speechless. "Colonel, darkness had fallen," he explained. "The Indian woman was hungry, and the horses had to be tended. When I found this campsite, dry and protected. . . ."

"Nevertheless," Sully broke in, "because of your actions, Sergeant Potter will be punished."

Cap hesitated before speaking. "What punishment did the sergeant earn by walking down here to talk to me, Colonel?"

"A month's pay," Sully replied. "And ten lashes for him and the sentry who let him pass."

"Ten lashes," Cap repeated, meeting the officer's gaze in the light of the campfire. "By whose authority?"

"The punishment to be meted out is my decision," Sully said. "We're in the field, and the punishment will serve as an example to other troopers. As a veteran of war, Mister McKenna, surely you understand that much."

"The war is over," Cap said.

"Not the war with the Indians," Sully countered.

Exasperated, Cap said: "As I recall military regulations, the accused may be confined, but not punished, until he stands before a court-martial."

"We are deployed in the field, sir," Sully snapped. "As commanding officer, I have authority to decide matters of discipline."

Cap saw the colonel square his shoulders.

"Sir," Tom Sully went on, "my estimation of you has changed a great deal. I do not believe you camped here by accident. I resent your tone of voice and the nature of your remarks. I am hereby serving you notice. If my troopers find you here tomorrow at first light, you will be subject to confinement and a military inquiry yourself."

"Sir?" Cap asked in disbelief.

"Defy my order," Sully said, "and you will face arrest for interfering with the discipline and morale of the men in my command."

Cap broke camp at dawn. He crossed the river with White Moon Woman close behind. At the wagon road, he led the way into a grove of cottonwoods, dismounted, and took the piebald's reins. White Moon Woman slid off the horse, watching Cap's face as she held her baby.

With hand signals and exaggerated gestures Cap attempted to explain that he would ride into town alone. He pointed to the path of the sun in the sky over the eastern horizon, trying to tell her that he would return in two hours or so. He left White Moon Woman squatting beside the piebald. He did not know if she understood, but he figured she was better off here than in town.

On the outskirts of Denver smoky fires marked crude camps by the river. Untold numbers of hungry men from gold camps in the mountains idly passed time here, men with no luck and few possessions other than the gear they carried in rucksacks. Cap knew from previous treks to Denver that many of these riverside camps were the domain of men who survived by thievery and strong-arm robbery. Of the thousands traveling to the territory in search of a new life in a new land, some were fleeing heinous crimes back in the States. They quickly discovered panning for gold was hard, miserable work, and turned to preying on settlers and miners and even on each other, prepared to kill or be killed in their search for riches or food for another day.

In town he tied his horse at the rail by the painted barber pole. He rolled a smoke and waited. The sun had eased up over the horizon. Presently the door opened and the owner, Dave, came out, broom in hand. A well-groomed man with salt-and-pepper hair and a bulging belly under his pinstriped vest, Dave methodically swept his section of the boardwalk between a hardware store and a laundry. Then he entered his shop, set the straw broom aside, and moved behind the big armchair.

Cap stepped into the doorway, awaiting an invitation. The barber stropped straight-edged razors until the blades were sharp enough to split a hair, and opened for business by putting on his apron. He jerked his head at Cap, first customer of the day.

After a trim, a shave, and a hot bath in the back room, Cap crossed the rutted street to the Rocky Mountain Café. The waitress who greeted him with a friendly smile had been hired since he last came here. A strong-looking, young woman with blonde hair in a French braid, she brought Cap the platter of ham and eggs he had ordered and then lingered for a brief conversation after pouring his coffee. Cap learned she had come here two months ago from Boston with her parents and two brothers who were now breaking ground south of town for a farm. When she learned that Cap owned cattle and land on Trapper Creek, she called him a rancher.

Cap felt his face warming from her friendly attentions, but, before he could ask her name, the sound of boots on the plank flooring outside drew her away from his table. Four cavalry officers trooped in for breakfast. The last was Major Symington.

Cap nodded when their eyes met, and the major came to his table.

"Morning, Mister McKenna," he said, taking off his hat.

"Call me Cap," he replied, standing.

Symington grinned and shook his hand. "The colonel let his liquor talk last night. Reckon you know he wouldn't have put you in irons, as he threatened."

"What about Sergeant Potter?" Cap asked.

"That's another matter entirely," Symington said, his smile fading.

"The sergeant is undeserving of a lashing."

"Sully's quick to punish. Every trooper in his command knows it."

"I'd like to speak to him today about the matter. . . ."

"Tom's not a man to cross," Symington warned. "I'd leave well enough alone, if you don't mind my saying so."

After breakfast Cap withdrew cash from his account in the

bank. He bought supplies at the false-fronted Hardware & Mining Supply, and then purchased box lunches next door from The Denver House.

Saddlebags bulging, Cap rode out of town. When the grove of cottonwoods came in sight, he stood in the stirrups. Sure enough, in a patch of shade ahead White Moon Woman waited with the baby and the piebald.

In the days after their return to the homestead on Trapper Creek, White Moon Woman stayed in sight of the cabin, but never ventured inside. Evenings she silently accepted the food Cap set out by his door. On these occasions he often held the baby while she ate.

Cap found pleasure in holding and playing with the infant. When he had been alone and solely responsible for the baby, he had felt the chill of gut-deep fear, an inner trembling that was new to him. After mother and child were reunited, the terror was lifted. Now Cap could enjoy these moments of play.

Most of White Moon Woman's time was spent in the aspen grove. For shade, she had fashioned a lean-to of woven branches cut with her skinning knife. Every morning at sunrise she greeted the new day, her face uplifted as she basked in the first golden light of the sun. She had made a trap of willows bound with wet bark, and snared several cottontails on the prairie. After skinning them, she cooked the meat over an open fire. She brought the tender meat to Cap, along with some root vegetables. Sometimes she presented him with trout caught by hand from the deepest pools of Trapper Creek.

Cap went about his chores, tending the stock and keeping the Reynolds outfits rolling. In their own ways, the two of them settled into a routine.

So he believed, until the day dawned when he did not hear

the usual cries of the baby from the stand of aspen trees. After breakfast Cap walked to the grove. Delicate aspen leaves, stirred by a breeze, fluttered like captive butterflies.

Kneeling, he looked into the small lean-to. The grass was matted where she had slept, but the army blanket was gone. He straightened. Turning, he listened and watched for several minutes. White Moon Woman had a way of standing motion-lessly, seeming to appear out of nowhere.

This time she did not appear. He left the grove and walked downslope to Trapper Creek. Scanning the bank, he searched for tracks in the soft soil. No sign of her there, either.

Chapter Six

Cap was unprepared for the loneliness that swept over him during the next several days. He discovered that he missed the wails of the infant. And he missed the company of White Moon Woman.

She had been a silent presence on the homestead, and more than once Cap had caught himself watching as she lugged water from Trapper Creek to her lean-to, or gathered wood for her fire. Sometimes her large dark eyes gazed his way, and across the open space between the log cabin and the aspen grove they looked at one another. After she left, Cap found himself continuing to glance toward the grove while going about his chores.

He wondered about White Moon Woman and her baby, but soon he was caught up in tumultuous events, one after another, and had little time for idle thoughts.

Three days after White Moon Woman left, Cap encountered soldiers on his homestead. A platoon of Ninth Cavalry was led by Major Luke Symington.

Tall and lean with a leathery tan, mounted, Symington looked every inch the cavalry officer. He rode fluidly, comfortable in a McClellan saddle as he leaned his weight into the stirrups, a man at ease on horseback. He hailed Cap with a wave and a shout.

Turning his buckskin, Cap met the column on the fire-blackened prairie. "What brings you out my way, Major?"

"My commanding officer reckons you know the reason," Symington replied.

Cap studied him.

"Well?" Symington said.

"This some parlor game?"

"No game," he replied. "Sergeant Joshua Potter is absent without leave."

Cap learned that Colonel Sully believed Potter had ridden to the homestead on Trapper Creek to find White Moon Woman. Symington's orders were to bring the sergeant back — along with the stolen horse, Spencer rifle, and Colt revolver, and all other gear issued by the U. S. government.

Cap answered the major's questions. He could only corroborate the date he last saw White Moon Woman. True, the time span was long enough for Potter to have made a hard ride here and taken her away in the night. But Cap had not heard or seen anything unusual the night of her disappearance. He had assumed she rejoined the band of Cheyennes she had traveled with — or perhaps the Indians had come for her.

The major regarded him. "My orders are to run Potter to ground and bring him in. Trackers followed the sergeant's horse this far." He paused, clearly uncomfortable.

Cap grinned. "You want to search my cabin and barn, don't you?"

Symington nodded. "Those are my orders."

Cap waved toward his homestead. "Search all you want, Major."

Cap watched him spur his mount and ride away. Crossing Trapper Creek, he rode to the barn doors, dismounted, and entered. In a few minutes he came out. After checking the cabin, he swung up and came back at a canter.

"Send out the trackers," he said to his sergeant as he reined up.

He turned to Cap. "Potter must have headed into the foothills. We'll cut his trail up there, likely."

The major's orders were passed along, and two trackers

62

spurred their horses. Cap recognized one. The short, stocky man was the sentry who had challenged him on the bank of the South Platte River. Their eyes met briefly as he rode away.

Symington muttered an apology to Cap, and then neck-reined his horse around. While Cap watched, the major led his detachment to the ridge beyond his homestead.

The next day a teamster, waving a newspaper over his head, brought shocking news — J. Stuart Reynolds was dead.

Reynolds was killed when his runaway team sent his buggy careening off a Chicago bridge. Cap read the newspaper article, recalling the matched black stallions he had seen under harness when Reynolds had visited out here.

"What will happen to the Reynolds Overland Transportation Company?"

That question was on the lips of every teamster who rolled into the homestead for a hot meal and a change of horses. Cap wondered, too. Two years remained on his contract with Reynolds. He did not know what would happen to his agreement, if the company was sold.

His life had taken a sharp turn into unknown territory the day he shook hands with J. Stuart Reynolds. He reflected on all that had happened in the last year, from nursing draft horses to chasing after them, to side-stepping a hoof or ducking equine teeth. If not for Reynolds, he would not have chased a runaway draft horse and found the baby wrapped in a blanket. That discovery had started a series of events he could never have foreseen.

Cap rolled a smoke. If he'd had a crystal ball to foretell the future, he might have declined the offer of a three-year contract with the Reynolds Overland Transportation Company. The promise of a barn had nudged him into the decision, and now he could lose it. If company assets were sold, the new owner could dismantle that barn and haul it away, log by log, on freight wagons when a crew came to take the draft horses and gear.

Cap touched a flame to the twisted end of the cigarette. He inhaled and blew out a cloud of smoke. Looking out across the prairie from his cabin, he wondered if he would change anything, after all. His feelings were jumbled. The horses had caused one problem after another, but he had enjoyed the company of the teamsters.

With troubles came certain pleasures. Cap thought about that. To his dying day he would remember the way the baby had stared at him when he unwrapped the army blanket that morning. Now, he wondered about White Moon Woman. And about Joshua Potter.

Rumors traveled by freight wagon over the next two weeks. Every teamster arrived with the latest rumor, or a new twist to an old one. First came word that the company had been sold and that all the assets would be auctioned. Then, no, the Reynolds Overland Transportation Company had not been sold. Reynolds, father to a daughter and son, was a long-time widower. Some said his children wanted to hold on to the freighting business. Then came rumors of bitter conflict. One partner in the company was intent on selling, while others wished to retain the business as a secure investment.

Truth was, Cap figured, no one outside the family knew what was going on. Maybe that Ashworth fellow, the attorney, did. But certainly no dust-eating teamster, popping a whip over a team of six, knew what was happening in the Chicago mansion of J. Stuart Reynolds.

Then the rumors died out. Cap heard no more about the future of Reynolds Overland — and no more about White Moon Woman and Joshua Potter, either. But one afternoon dust rising far out on the burned prairie caught his eye. No wind blew. It was not a dust devil. The haze hung in the sky like a soiled cloud.

Cap figured the dust was raised by Symington's column of cavalry returning to Denver. He wondered if the major had captured Potter. No way to find out, short of riding to Denver and asking Colonel Tom Sully if the sergeant was in custody.

A week later Cap was in his barn, tending horses, when he heard splashes coming from the creek. His ears told him it was not a freight wagon, but the clatter of a lighter vehicle. He moved down the runway to the doors and stepped out of the barn. A covered surrey rolled to a stop in front of the cabin.

Cap crossed the yard, coming up behind the surrey. The driver set the brake and climbed out. He was young, Cap noticed, a boy of twelve or thirteen, fair-haired, with a sun-blistered nose. The youth grinned broadly, lifting his new drover's hat in greeting.

"Mister McKenna!"

Cap met him by the rear wheel of the vehicle. He shook the outstretched hand, wondering where he had seen that boyish grin before. Even the voice rang a bell in his memory, yet he knew he had never met this boy before.

"Don't believe we've met," Cap said.

"No, sir. My father told me about you."

"Your father," Cap repeated.

The surrey creaked. Cap turned and saw a woman's lace-up shoe on the step plate.

"Sis, you need a hand?"

"No."

Cap watched a young woman climb out, her down-turned face hidden by a hat brim until both feet were on the ground.

"Good evening, Mister McKenna," she said, raising her

head. She smiled. "My name is Jane Reynolds. This is my brother, Jamie."

Cap stared — first at her, then at the sun-burned boy. Reynolds. Now he recognized the squared face and a certain eagerness in the wide-set eyes.

"Your father," he said slowly, "is . . . was J. Stuart Reynolds."

"Yes, sir!" Jamie replied.

Cap offered condolences to the son and daughter of the famous man. His gaze lingered on Jane. No more than two or three years older than her brother, he figured she was sixteen or seventeen. Slender and pretty with her long, sandy hair pinned back, she wore a maroon dress under the ankle-length duster that she unbuttoned now.

"We apologize for appearing out of the blue on your doorstep," she said.

"We took the train from Chicago to Cheyenne," Jamie chimed in, "and then a stagecoach south to Denver. I got seasick from all that rocking back and forth, back and forth."

Jane put her arm around his shoulders. "In Denver we bought supplies and rented this rig and team."

An awkward silence followed. Cap was baffled. He could not understand why they were here, but figured this visit had something to do with Reynolds Overland.

Cap cleared his throat. "Miss Reynolds . . . ?"

"Please call me Jane," she broke in with a smile.

"Jane," he said, "all the men are wondering . . . well, they're wondering what'll happen to Reynolds Overland now that . . . ?"

When she offered no answer to his implied question, Cap went on: "Rumors are going around about the company being sold . . . ?"

"Reynolds wagons are still hauling freight," she interrupted.

Looking past him, Jane drew a deep breath. "Daddy was right. Just look at that view, Jamie . . . God's country, as pure and fine as the day the earth began."

"Daddy told us all about the frontier," Jamie said, "and about meeting you. That's why we chose this place."

"Chose this place," Cap repeated slowly.

Jane gestured to the mountains behind the cabin. "Jamie and I want to explore. We want to roam freely through forests and meadows, climb the highest mountain, sip the chilled waters of ancient glaciers. We want to set foot where only the silent, soft-soled moccasin has bent grasses and nudged brilliant flowers blooming in wild profusion."

Cap stared while she delivered this speech. "Yes, ma'am, a feller has to be careful where he walks."

"Oh, I know you're humoring me," she said. "I was reciting the words of a visionary essayist who wrote about the mountains beyond the prairie. His words are sheer poetry. Daddy read them aloud to us. This is the land we want to explore. We want to see it, smell it, taste it . . . experience pristine nature, first-hand."

Cap held back a smile.

Jamie added: "We won't cause you any trouble, Mister McKenna. We brought everything we'll need." He leaned into the surrey and opened a canvas-covered compartment behind the seat. Amid the hard leather luggage, Cap observed a number of wooden boxes containing tins of meat and fruit and cotton sacks of rice and dried beans. Camp pans and utensils, a lantern, coal oil, rucksacks, and canteens were stashed under the seat.

Cap gestured to his cabin. "You're welcome to stay here."

After helping Jamie carry the luggage into the cabin, he drove the surrey to the barn and unhooked the team. Jamie came along and helped feed and rub down the horses. The boy was unfamiliar with simple chores, Cap noticed, but he was eager to please.

At sundown Cap stoked the stove while his guests sat on the bunk, watching. He roasted and ground coffee beans. When Jane moved to his side and offered to help, he handed her a bag of lemons brought by a teamster.

As she halved and squeezed them for lemonade, Cap warmed some beans while thick slices of bacon popped and curled in the black iron skillet. He dropped in spoonfuls of cornmeal batter. The cabin filled with the smells of food cooking and coffee brewing.

Jane and Jamie ate hungrily, awarding the meal extravagant praise. Stirring sugar into her tin cup of lemonade, Jane observed that food tasted better out here in the Wild West than back home.

After supper, Cap shook out the blanket on his bunk. "I'll bed down in the barn."

"Oh, no," Jane protested. "We will not drive you from your home."

Cap insisted he would be comfortable in the barn, saying Reynolds teamsters often used the bunk in the tack room. It was only practical for two people to sleep in the cabin.

Jane relented, but only for temporary quarters, she said, adding that they had not come all this way to sleep in a cabin.

"We want to slumber under twinkling Western stars," she said, "and gaze at the silver moon in a hard black sky."

"Same stars out here," Cap said, "as the ones twinkling over Chicago."

"Oh, I know," she said, flashing a self-conscious smile. "But life is richer, fuller without the trappings of civilization, don't you think? Oh, I do. The essayist wrote about waters flowing diamond clear, the air smelling as fresh as the day the earth began. No fumes from coal smoke, no foul, hissing steam engines, no clank or rattle from a passing trolley."

"Reckon so," Cap said, "but we get lightning storms out here that'll stand your hair on end."

Jane sipped her lemonade, her eyes blinking rapidly. "Daddy was right, Mister McKenna. This is God's country. I feel Daddy's presence . . . as though he's looking down from the heavens . . . watching over us right now."

In the next three days Jane and Jamie hiked over the ridge behind the cabin, returning each afternoon at sunset. To meet nature head-on, Jane wore a high-collar jacket, white cotton blouse with a divided skirt, and lace-up boots. She pinned her hair up under a felt hat. Jamie was dressed in canvas trousers, a duck coat over his flannel shirt, new boots, and that out-sized, wide-brimmed hat — purchases made in Denver.

Cap watched the pair leave the cabin every morning, Jane a head taller than her brother. Shouldering rucksacks, they hiked side by side up the slope of the ridge. In the early eve-ning they returned, tired and sweating, both welcoming a hot meal and a mug of coffee.

Each night they also nursed blisters from their new foot-gear. Jane was pestered by bites from mosquitoes and deer flies, and had tied a scarf around her head to protect her face. Jamie wore a blue bandanna around his neck after the fashion of cattle drovers he had seen in Denver. His nose had turned tomato red, and Cap applied horse liniment to the sunburned, blistering skin.

Exhausted, the two of them retired early every evening. Jane slept on the bunk, while Jamie made his bed on the floor.

They did not discuss their discoveries or share their inspi-rations while communing with nature. Cap had warned them about encountering bears and cougars or even an aggressive bull on his tree claim, and he figured that now the reality of surviving in a wilderness made them seek the safety of his cabin every day at sundown.

He soon discovered he was wrong. They had a plan. The pair lugged food, cooking gear, a hand axe, and canteens of water to an unknown destination, and returned with empty rucksacks.

Remaining mystified by their presence, Cap did not ask questions. On the frontier, questioning a back trail was bad manners. The sister and brother did not ask about his background, either, apparently trusting him solely because their father had hired him.

For himself, Cap had buried the past. He never spoke of his time in the war. Talk would only dig up pain and anguish, and breathe new life into old horrors. No volume of Civil War history would record that sunny April morning in 1865 when Company B had sauntered into a Confederate ambush. Within seconds eleven men lay dead or dying on an oak-lined country lane, some with boots tangled in stirrups and dragged by their squealing, injured horses. Seven more cavalrymen had suffered painful deaths in a field hospital. The confederate bullets had missed Cap. His horse had sunk under him. He had leaped from the dying animal, and had scrambled behind a stone fence. He had returned fire until the ambushers withdrew.

Never diagrammed on a military map or studied by historians, that bloody ambush on the eve of victory was known only to the survivors — and to one battlefield captain who wrote letters to the families of the dead. Cap had taken those memories home with him. The men of his command had been young, but they had been veterans, well armed and confident. That day on the peaceful country lane all of them had been buoyed by a growing certainty that the war was nearing an end.

Ever since, the vision of dead and dying men lived on in Cap's dreams, as though his mind struggled to alter the outcome. When he had worked on his father's rented field after mustering out, tears had mixed with sweat. Cap had pulled a bandanna from his hip pocket and wiped his face, his broad shoulders quaking.

His dreams haunted by war, Edwin Horatio McKenna had not known what he had wanted from life until he had seen a public notice tacked on a wall in the post office. He had read the provisions of the Homestead Act that had been signed into law by President Lincoln. The frontier and its promise of land had beckoned, and, like many other veterans, he had answered the call.

Chapter Seven

"Good bye, Cap."

He shook hands with Jane and Jamie, and watched them leave the cabin. They crossed the grassy flat and headed upslope toward the forested ridge, both of them limping on tender feet. He figured their camp was not far away, close enough to allow them to come running back, if aid and shelter were needed.

The next afternoon Cap had dumped a bucket of water into the trough by the corral, when a rumble of thunder drew his gaze skyward. Dark clouds swelled into domed thunderheads over the Rocky Mountains. He saw a flash of lightning stab out of the black underbelly, and the air grew hot and still.

Rainstorm coming, he thought, *and hail, maybe.*

Cap jogged to the barn. He yanked open the doors. Hurrying back to the corral, he opened the gate and herded the two livery horses toward the barn. Thunder and lightning had made the critters nervous, and now the dark opening of the barn doorway spooked them. They tried to flee, but Cap got the jump on them. He side-stepped, waving his hat and whistling, as he turned them and drove them inside.

He left the two horses milling in the barn's runway, closed the doors, and stepped outside. Standing under the overhang of the roof, he pulled the makings out of his shirt pocket and rolled a smoke.

Raindrops raised dust on the dry earth minutes before the downpour began. When it came, heavy rain fell for a quarter of an hour. Then hail dropped out of the sky like white marbles, each one frozen hard enough to rebound two feet into the air after striking the ground.

Cap shoved his hat back on his head. He knelt, listening to hailstones pound the barn's shake roof like a monotonous drum roll. At his feet rivulets of dark brown mud gathered in pools that spilled over into miniature floods.

As Cap expected, the storm was short-lived. Wind-driven black clouds stampeded eastward over the prairie like a herd of airborne beasts. The hail abruptly stopped. The rain let up. Moments later the sun came out, shining brightly in a widening patch of blue sky.

Cap stepped away from the protection of the overhang. Hailstones lay in tufts of wet grass like half-hidden pearls. He found Trapper Creek churning with muddy water. Returning to the barn, he opened the doors and herded the livery horses back into the corral.

Cap's prediction about the weather had been right, but he guessed wrong about Jane and Jamie Reynolds. He figured the storm would drive them out of the forest straight to his cabin. But they did not come running back to safety that day, and they weathered another fierce rainstorm the next afternoon, too.

A day later Dud Dawkins arrived. While changing horses, he spotted the surrey beside the barn and asked Cap about his guests. Dud had turned to spit, but his head snapped around when he heard their names.

"Who?" the teamster demanded, tobacco juice trickling down his chin.

"Jane and Jamie Reynolds," Cap repeated. "Daughter and son of J. Stuart Reynolds."

"Well, I'll be damned," he said, wiping his beard-stubbled chin with the back of his hand. "What's gonna come of Reynolds Overland?"

"Wish I knew."

73

"Didn't they tell you nothing?"

"Jane Reynolds said the wagons are rolling, and that's all she said."

Dud considered that. "Well, what're they doing out here?"

"Exploring nature."

"Huh?"

Cap waved toward the ridge. "They made a camp somewhere over yonder. They're planning to climb a mountain."

"Just that . . . climb up some damned mountain?"

Cap nodded.

"Prospecting for gold?"

Cap shook his head.

Dud stared at him. "What's this damned world coming to?"

The next day another Reynolds' teamster rolled in, stopping long enough for a noon meal and fresh team. Denver-bound with a load of millinery goods under the canvas — notions, bolts of fabric, needles and spools of thread, ladies' hats and high button shoes — the teamster washed his face in the trough and then drank a mug of coffee before climbing up to the wagon seat. He popped his long-handled whip, departing with a wave.

In the evening Cap was in his cabin scrubbing his skillet with a handful of sand from the streambed when he heard saddle horses splash through Trapper Creek. He stepped outside, wiping his hands on the cotton flour sack he used for a towel.

Three riders trotted into the yard, their mounts' hoofs tossing wet clods. The men wore mud-splattered dusters with the collars turned up and narrow-brimmed city hats. Rifles were in their saddle scabbards. The smallest of the trio hunched forward in his saddle and peered through spectacles.

"McKenna!"

Cap looked at the man who called out, seeing gray eyes magnified by steel-rimmed lenses — Stanley Ashworth. Flanking him were the same riders who had accompanied J. Stuart Reynolds and the attorney on their first visit to the homestead.

"Howdy, Mister Ashworth," Cap replied. "Step down."

Ashworth made no move to dismount. "Where are they, McKenna?"

Cap eyed him.

"Despite rumors you may have heard," Ashworth said, "you have no cause to shelter or conceal Jane and young Jamie."

The remark surprised Cap. "No one's hiding here."

"McKenna, do not lie to me."

Cap dropped the towel and moved closer, fists clenched. "Mister, climb down off that horse and call me a liar."

The gunmen reached for their rifles, stopping when Ashworth raised his hand.

"We'll see who is telling the truth, McKenna. You're acquainted with a teamster named Dawkins . . . Dudley Dawkins?"

Cap did not reply.

"I spoke to Mister Dawkins in Cheyenne," Ashworth went on, "and he told me you readily admitted Jane and Jamie were guests here on your homestead. Sir, I do not want a fight. I want the truth."

"Truth is," Cap said, meeting his gaze, "I don't know where they are. It's none of my business."

"If I informed you the future of Reynolds Overland depended on your answer, would you still make that claim?"

"What're you getting at?"

"As attorney for the Reynolds family, I am required to maintain confidentiality. All I can tell you is that I must speak to Jane and Jamie right away. I assure you, McKenna, their best interests will be served, if you cooperate." He added: "So will yours."

At sunup the four of them rode out with Cap leading the way. Last night Ashworth had slept in the tack room, his hired gunmen taking turns standing watch at the barn doors. They had been introduced by their first names — the big one was Archie, the slender man, Leonard.

Cap urged his horse up the slope behind the cabin toward the heavy timber. Reaching the bench, he glanced over his shoulder. The three men had dropped back, their livery horses already fatigued.

He let the buckskin pick a route through the thick ponderosas, and topped the crest. Breaking out of the pines on the other side, he reined up. Two dozen cattle lined the creek, grazing in high grass near the place where he had found the baby. Now the cows lifted their heads, eyeing him. Several backed away. When one wheeled, all of them trotted into the trees.

Cap held a tight rein as the buckskin's urge for the chase made him prance. The three riders caught up, their horses breathing hard from the climb.

Cap rode slowly along the bank of the gurgling creek. He leaned over the horn as he searched for trampled grass and footprints in the mud. He saw a variety of tracks — deer, elk, bear, cougar, coyote, raccoon, skunk, birds — but no human sign, until he had ridden nearly a hundred yards downstream. Then he saw a boot print.

Nearby tracks of a shod horse were pressed deeply into the mud. He looked around and then studied the boot print. It was too large and too heavy to have been left by either Jane or Jamie.

Joshua Potter, Cap guessed, and backed his horse over the

tracks. The depth of the horse tracks indicated Potter and White Moon Woman were riding double.

"Well?" Ashworth said, moving up beside him.

"No sign along here," Cap said, noticing the man made no attempt to read tracks in the mud. He was uneasy about Stanley Ashworth, and as yet undecided about how far he would go to co-operate with him.

Ashworth adjusted his spectacles and looked around. "Which way could they have gone?"

Cap scanned the shadowed timber. This day was turning warm with the sun's heat drawing the resin smell out of the pine pitch. A bluejay called from a nearby treetop, and flew away. If they were determined, Cap realized now, Jane and her brother could have hiked a fair distance from here. He recalled her comment about making camp in a mountain valley. At the time he figured they would not range far from his cabin. Now he suspected he had underestimated them.

Shifting his hips in the saddle, Cap gestured to a mountain due west. Ashworth shaded his eyes from the bright sky as he looked in that direction. The distant peak was marked by an escarpment of gray granite where fractured stone stretched skyward, a wide and sheer cliff streaked by snow.

"If they headed that way," Cap said, "they probably took the easiest route they could find."

Ashworth gave him a skeptical look. "Guesswork . . . is that the best you can do?"

"Mister Ashworth," Cap replied, "if you don't want my guesswork, I'll ride home."

Ashworth gestured ahead impatiently. "All right, all right. Get on with it. Lead the way."

Jaw clenched, Cap reined the buckskin around. He splashed across the stream, heading into thick timber. He was familiar with the immediate area from tracking cattle through forests and over ridges every autumn. But by mid-afternoon, when he topped a rock-strewn ridge, he had journeyed deeper into the mountains than he had ever been before. Still he had not cut sign.

Dismounting, he led his horse through the loose rock. The buckskin slipped and bumped against him, almost knocking him down. Man and horse staggered, regained their balance, and went on with the three men cautiously following.

Cap thought again about the distance Jane and Jamie might have hiked. Traveling on foot had some advantages over riding a horse. In rugged country a hiker with a rucksack could scale rocks and vault over downed timber. On horseback, the rider had to find routes his mount could traverse without balking or breaking a leg, and this led to frequent backtracking in search of a path around natural obstacles.

Cap found the far side of the ridge too steep to be passable. He led the way along the crest for two hundred yards. In open ground near a stand of lodgepole pines the slope was gentle. He swung up and guided his horse in a zigzag path down the side of the ridge. The lodgepoles were thin and straight trees, evenly spaced like teeth in a comb.

A distant roar reached him. Mist came into the air, cooling his face. Through a break in the pines he saw a small waterfall in the valley below. There a turquoise pool churned white bubbles.

Cap watched a shadow sweep over the land, silent and fast, and he looked up. A hawk circled high in the blue sky. Pausing long enough for Ashworth to catch up, he watched the winged hunter swoop down into the valley, flying low over the water. From here the stream ran through grass and wildflowers like a shiny ribbon.

After leading the way to the valley floor, Cap followed the stream past a string of beaver ponds, each with a dome-shaped lodge of mud and sticks where the animals lived. Aspen stumps gnawed to a point by beavers lined the banks along this stretch. Generations of beavers had backed up water in their network of dams, creating a swampy marsh. As Cap rode past the ponds, wild ducks took flight, angling upward with a panicked thrashing of their wings.

Farther downstream the creek meandered into a wide meadow where it looped back and forth in a maze of semi-circles nearly hidden by chest-high willows. Riding clear of the marsh, Cap guided his horse into this meadow and reined up. In the grass he saw circles of round stones — teepee rings. He knew Indians used river rocks to hold down the bottom edges of their teepees.

Cap looked around. He spotted stones blackened by fires, but saw no recent signs — no bent grass, no animal droppings, no ashes or bones — none of the leavings of nomadic tribes. At some time in the past Indians must have cut lodgepoles from the forest on the mountainside and made summer camp here. But not this season.

He swung down. At the creek he refilled his canteen. Ashworth and the two men reined up behind him, dismounted, and walked stiff-legged to the creek. They dropped to their knees and drank thirstily, and then stretched out on the ground to rest.

Cap watched them. They had not spotted the teepee rings — or if they did, they failed to understand the significance of circles of rocks in the grass. These men were out of their element, Cap thought again. He knew it was not unusual for a city man to hire gunmen while traveling in the West. The law was stretched thin in the territories, and armed guards gave a man of means some security. Now Cap noticed that both men kept a wary eye on him, clearly under orders to prevent him from committing some treachery against them.

Leonard was a strange one. He seemed to enjoy watching Cap while twirling a bone-handled Bowie knife. Thin lips under his beak-like nose sometimes curled into a smile as he stared wordlessly, the blade of his big knife mirroring the sunlight.

Archie was a slow beast of a man. Beard and hair matted with sweat, his mouth now hung open from the day's exertion. But he remained alert even as he reclined in the grass, his Winchester close by.

Half an hour later Ashworth stood. Cap took the hint and got to his feet. He strode to his grazing horse, tightened the saddle cinch, and swung up. When the others were mounted, he led the way out of the meadow on a well-worn trail left by deer and elk.

"Now where're you taking us?" Ashworth demanded, kicking his horse to catch up.

Cap turned in the saddle. "If Jane and Jamie came this way, I figure they followed the game trail up the side of that mountain."

"Can't you find tracks?" Ashworth demanded.

"Two people on foot don't leave much of a trail," Cap replied. "Seems to me they've been careful."

Ashworth shook his head in a hopeless gesture. "We could wander through this god-forsaken terrain for weeks."

Cap rode on. He had hoped to spot footprints in the soft ground, catch the scent of woodsmoke, or come across discarded tins — some sort of sign. All morning he had scanned the stands of trees, alert for the fresh slashes of a hand axe. Jane had mentioned constructing a shelter, and cuts on a tree would catch his eye.

He did not say so, but Ashworth was right. Jane and Jamie could have veered off to the north or south, and, by now, they could be anywhere within a two-day hike from the ridge behind his cabin. But as he recalled Jane's comment about climbing the highest mountain, he figured they had headed this way.

The game trail led toward a stand of thick-trunked ponderosa pines. Approaching the ancient forest, Cap spotted movement in the shadows. In the next instant the buckskin tossed his head and pranced.

He drew rein and peered ahead. White Moon Woman stepped out of the trees. Holding her baby, she lifted her hand to Cap in greeting.

"Indians!" Ashworth shouted. "Indians!"

Cap heard dry clicks as rifle hammers were cocked. He whirled around in time to see Archie and Leonard raise their weapons to their shoulders.

Cap pulled the right rein and kneed his horse, at once yelling: "Don't shoot!"

His horse wheeled, but Cap was too late. Squinting over their gunsights, Archie and Leonard fired in quick succession. The loud reports roared through Cap's ears as he charged them.

Chapter Eight

Cap reached out with his free hand and grabbed the barrel of Archie's rifle. Yanking it from him, he flung the weapon away, kicked his horse, and went after Leonard. The smaller man tried to pull his mount back, but the frightened animal reared.

With a cavalryman's instincts, Cap closed in. He had no saber, but he managed to grab the sleeve of Leonard's duster as the wild-eyed horse came down. Spurring the buckskin again, he jerked Leonard out of the saddle and sent him tumbling to earth.

Cap rode around in a half circle, his gaze searching the treeline. He feared he would spot a body sprawled on the ground, and was relieved when he saw that White Moon Woman was not there.

"What . . . ?" Ashworth demanded, his mouth twisting with rage. "What in the name of hell are you doing?"

"Stopping your men from murdering a mother and her baby," Cap replied.

He reined his horse to a halt beside Ashworth. An angry Leonard staggered to his feet, bringing his gun up. Archie had dismounted and retrieved his rifle.

"I oughta shoot you out of your saddle!" Leonard shouted, levering a fresh round into the chamber.

Cap reached for his holstered revolver.

"Give the word, Mister Ashworth," Archie added as he aimed his gun at Cap. "Just give the word."

Cap's hand closed around the grips of his Colt when Ashworth intervened.

"Lower those guns . . . now! Save your ammunition. That forest is full of savages, ready to attack. . . ."

"I don't think so," Cap broke in.

Ashworth drew a breath. "Well now, McKenna, exactly what do you think?"

Cap ignored Ashworth's sarcasm. "I don't believe that woman is with a tribe."

"You know her?"

"Wait here," he said, and touched spurs to his horse.

"McKenna . . . ?"

Cap did not look back. He guided the buckskin to the spot where he had last seen White Moon Woman. He studied the ground, relieved again when no blood was visible on the green blades of grass. He rode into the forest at a walk, making his way through the stand of towering ponderosas. Sun-sifted shadows stretched out before him in a dark maze. A chill ran up his spine.

He hoped he was right — that White Moon Woman was alone and had not rejoined a tribe. He saw nothing to alarm him, but knew warriors could be concealed close at hand, nearly invisible, and, after Archie and Leonard had fired their rifles, they would not be friendly.

He angled to open ground along the bank of the creek and searched the mud and sand for fifty yards. Spotting boot prints at the water's edge, he reined up and swung down. The tracks were left by large riding boots, matching the single print he had seen on his tree claim. These were fresh. Water seeped into the deeper imprints left by the heel.

"Stand!"

Startled, Cap straightened up.

"Keep your hands out where I can see them!"

He turned slowly. "Potter."

Joshua Potter rose up from the thick brush, a Spencer carbine clenched in his hands. He stepped out of the thicket. Cap saw that he wore cavalry trousers and boots, a battered campaign hat, and a civilian shirt of gray flannel.

"Symington's patrol missed you," Cap observed.

Potter moved closer, studying him. "You scouting for the Army, Cap?"

"No," he replied, and recounted his unexpected meeting with Symington on the prairie. "The major was determined to bring you in."

"Cavalry makes too much racket to catch White Moon Woman," Potter said with half a grin. "Cap, I done ended my enlistment. The ol' man, he put the lash to me like I wasn't nothing but his slave. Soon's I got my strength up, I made my break. Took a horse, gear, and weapons because the ol' man whupped me and fined me a month of wages I done earned." After a brief pause, he added: "I knowed where Trapper Creek was, and followed it to your homestead."

Potter turned. He lifted his hand in a signal. White Moon Woman stepped out of the trees. Baby in her arms, she moved to Potter's side and cast a tentative smile at Cap.

"I didn't wake you that night I came for her," Potter went on, "so as not to cause trouble. Figured you couldn't say nothing to white officers, if you didn't know nothing."

Cap watched him put his arm around White Moon Woman's shoulders. He said: "I'm the one who brought on the trouble. You took that whipping because of me."

"No, suh, that wasn't your doing," Potter said, shaking his head. "No, suh. You brung my son to me, that's what you done. Ever' damned lash of that whip made me remember my son. Gave me strength. Yes, suh." Potter gestured toward the meadow. "Who's the trigger-happy gents you're riding with . . . huntin' party?"

Cap shook his head. He told him about Ashworth. "The

84

man asked my help in locating the camp of a sister and brother. So far I haven't cut sign. . . ."

"Young woman and a boy?" Potter broke in. "Both of 'em on foot?"

Cap stared at him. "You've seen them?"

"White Moon Woman done spotted 'em," he said. He pointed toward the mountainside. "The young 'uns, they's holed up in a cave up there."

"Will you take us to them?"

Potter paused. "I don't want horsebackers milling around here. I'm building a lean-to back there in the trees while White Moon Woman's drying venison for jerky and pounding meat and berries for pemmican. A trail of shod hoofs will give away our camp, if Symington comes back."

"You aim to winter here?"

He nodded. "Me and White Moon Woman, we'll never be married, not in no Bible way. But we'll make a home, and we'll raise that boy. For now we'll lay low till the snow flies, and the Army moves on.

"Seems Cheyennes used this here area for summer hunting grounds. White Moon Woman found a cache of bows and arrows and some flint cutting tools. I finally figured out what she was trying to tell me about this place. The band that came here was wiped out in their winter camp on the Washita River by Custer's troopers."

Potter drew a deep breath. "Dunno how to put it into the right words, Cap, but when I see teepee rings out there, I see the Indian wars in a different light . . . and I don't much like what I see. That's why I don't want a trail leading to our camp."

Cap said: "If we leave our horses in the meadow and hike to the cave, there will be no trail."

While Potter considered that, Cap added: "The sooner

85

Ashworth delivers his message to Jane and Jamie, the sooner he'll head back to Chicago."

Joshua Potter glanced at White Moon Woman. Then he nodded.

In the meadow Cap introduced Ashworth to Potter. White Moon Woman had stayed behind with the baby, out of sight in the forest. Cap assured Ashworth no warriors lay in ambush there.

Ashworth's doubts were overcome by his excitement upon learning Potter knew where Jane and Jamie had gone. But when Cap announced they would hike on foot to the cave on the mountainside, he pulled Cap aside.

"That colored man is with the Indian woman?" he asked in a low voice.

Cap nodded.

"What if they have devised a scheme?"

"Scheme?" Cap repeated.

"She steals our horses and gear," he said, "while he leads us on some wild goose chase."

Cap studied him.

"Well?"

"I'm trying to figure it out."

"Figure what out?"

"If all city men are suspicious like you."

Ashworth's face hardened.

"They aren't thieves," Cap assured him. "I'm leaving my cow horse hobbled here by the creek . . . along with my rifle and saddlebags."

"You trust them?"

"More than those two jugheads you're riding with."

"All right, all right. We'll hike. But my men will be armed."

With the horses stripped and hobbled in the high grass,

the five of them walked single file out of the meadow. They waded the creek to a game trail leading to the base of the mountain. Cap and Potter made their way through the brush to a jumble of rocks deposited from an ancient landslide. The trail zigzagged through boulders up the mountain.

After half an hour Ashworth and his men had dropped back, all three breathing hard through open mouths, their faces shining with sweat. Archie and Leonard were weighted down by their rifles and cartridge belts. Ashworth walked gimpily on sore feet.

Cap's feet hurt, too, from walking in boots made for the stirrup. He halted, and so did Potter. Sitting side by side on a flat boulder, they watched the city men stagger as they made their way up the steep trail.

"That lawyer man must have a powerful reason for finding them young 'uns," Potter said, "to suffer like he is."

Cap nodded agreement. He disliked Ashworth, but had no reason to steer him away from Jane and Jamie. After the message was delivered, he had decided, he would escort him and the gunmen back to his homestead and send them on their way.

Cap looked around. Single trees grew randomly here, like spears launched by a giant warrior. Far below, the creek slid over a rocky bed and disappeared in the dark forest. When Ashworth and his men caught up, they sat heavily and wiped their brows, then drank from their canteens.

The ascent took another quarter of an hour. Potter halted and pointed to a formation of white stone in the gray granite fifty yards above them. In the middle was a dark semi-circle — the mouth of a large cave. The massive quartz outcropping was frost white, the cave black as coal.

"Cheyenne elders claim it's home to spirits," Potter said. "So says White Moon Woman."

"You speak her language?" Cap asked.

"Some," Potter said. "We do our talking with hand signs, making faces, and a few words here and there. Usually I get some notion of her meaning. Like that cave. Near as I can figure, she says it opens into the beating heart of the mountain." He asked: "You believe in spirits?"

"I'm inclined to be respectful of the unknown."

"Yes, suh," Potter replied, chuckling. "Yes, suh."

Well ahead of the city men, they climbed over the rocks to the quartz formation. Cap found the cave to be half the size of a barn when he stepped into its cool darkness.

Potter moved beside him. "Big, ain't it?"

Cap nodded and slowly walked into the cave.

"Cold, too, like an ice box," Potter said.

"Or tomb," Cap said and shivered.

The cave walls narrowed. Cap kicked an object that rolled away and rang with a hollow, metallic clatter. He knelt. Groping around, his fingers touched an empty tin. He picked it up and held it to the light. Still sticky from juice, the can had contained pears.

As their eyes adjusted, they found unopened tins of food, cooking utensils, and canteens corked and full of water. Moving toward the rear wall of the cave, they discovered clothing, neatly folded and stacked on the ground.

Cap sensed more than saw the back wall. Holding out his hands, he touched a cold, rough surface. He turned back.

"Wonder where them young 'uns went," Potter said, when they returned to sunlight at the mouth of the cave.

Cap looked out over the forested ridges due east, trying to spot his tree claim from here. Then directly below, movement caught his eye. He saw a furry marmot lying in the sunshine on the flat surface of a rock.

"Too cold to stay in here all day," Potter added. "Maybe

they's out exploring, warmed by the sun like that critter." Potter had smiled when he saw the animal. As big as a house cat, it lumbered away when Ashworth and the two gunmen reached the cave mouth.

The attorney's temper flared. He expected to find Jane and Jamie, and, after peering into the cold and empty shadows, he slapped his hands together in frustration.

"Now what?" he demanded.

"All their supplies are here," Cap said. "We can wait for them to come back, or hike some more if you want to continue to search."

Ashworth swore. He sat down, grimacing, and yanked off his hat. The two gunmen positioned themselves to the left and right of Cap, pulled off their boots, and massaged sore feet.

"Thank you for your assistance, Mister Potter," Ashworth said, dismissing him with a wave of his hand. "Your services are no longer required."

After a moment the lawyer added: "I can offer payment. . . ."

"I don't want your money, suh."

"All right then," Ashworth said. "You may leave."

Potter exchanged an eye-rolling glance with Cap. He moved out of the cave entrance and started downslope.

Cap went after him. Below the mouth of the cave he shook his hand and offered a word of thanks.

"Watch 'em," Potter whispered, "watch 'em close."

Cap climbed back to the cave. Finding a comfortable boulder, he sat down and rolled and smoked a cigarette. Then he stood and stretched his sore legs. A long hour stretched into two. At last, looking down from the mouth of the cave, he saw movement far below. He leaned forward.

Two figures emerged from the brush growing like a beard

at the base of the rockslide. Jane and Jamie began stair-stepping in their upward climb, unseen by Ashworth and his hired men until Cap spoke.

Ashworth rushed to his side. He peered down the mountainside where Cap pointed.

"Move back!" the lawyer exclaimed. "Move back!"

Cap began: "I'll wait out here where it's warm. . . ."

"No, you won't," Ashworth said.

Hearing a new tone in his voice, Cap turned. He saw a small pistol in his hand. Leonard, standing off to the left, leveled his rifle at him now, chest high. Archie moved up behind Cap and yanked the revolver from his holster.

"Do as you're told," Ashworth said. "Now."

Chapter Nine

Cap stepped into the cave. "Just what do you aim to do to those youngsters?"

"McKenna, you strike me as a man unaccustomed to taking orders," Ashworth said. "I admire your sense of independence. But here's some good advice . . . mind to your own affairs, and you will come out of this experience with nothing more than injured pride."

"In other words," Leonard said, "shut your damned mouth and keep it shut."

Archie added: "Or something besides your pride will get injured."

After a long wait the sound of Jamie's voice reached the height of the cave. Ashworth shoved his pistol into the shoulder holster and turned his attention to the mouth of the cave.

Cap, too, heard the boy talking to his sister, complaining of mosquito bites, as they climbed. Moments later they appeared at the cave opening.

Jane gasped, halting when she saw the four men. She reached out and grabbed Jamie. Her gaze darted past the gunmen to Cap, and then to Ashworth when he spoke.

"Hello, Jane." When she did not reply, he admonished the siblings: "You should have talked to me before you left Chicago in the night. . . ."

Jane shook her head vigorously. "I . . . I have nothing to say to you, Mister Ashworth."

"To the contrary, we have much to discuss regarding your financial well-being."

"Get out! Go away!" Jamie blurted. "Leave us alone!"

Ashworth ignored the boy and held his gaze on Jane. "After we have fully discussed the financial implications of your decision regarding Reynolds Overland, you may do whatever you wish."

"Mister Ashworth," Jane said, her chest heaving, "please . . . leave us alone."

"After I have explained. . . ."

"Get out!" Jamie yelled again. "You bastard!"

This time he caught the lawyer's attention. "Now, you listen to me. . . ."

Cap moved a step closer. "Leave them be."

Face flushed, Ashworth waved a hand at Archie and Leonard. "Gentlemen, escort Mister McKenna to the horses."

Cap backed up a step, fists clenched.

"Don't be a fool," Ashworth said with a sidelong glance at him. The gunmen aimed their rifles at him now. "What can you possibly hope to achieve against these odds?"

"Stop!" Jane shouted, her voice cracking. "All of you! Stop!"

Ashworth turned to her in surprise.

"Mister McKenna, please leave with those two men," Jane said, taking shallow, quick breaths. "Jamie and I . . . we'll speak to Mister Ashworth."

"Ah, the voice of common sense," Ashworth said. "Do as the young lady asks, McKenna . . . now."

"I will," Cap said, "when you hand over that little pistol."

"Hand it over," Ashworth repeated. "To you? What do you take me for?"

"You don't want to know," Cap replied.

Anger narrowed the lawyer's eyes.

"I don't care who you give that gun to," Cap went on. "With your good intentions, you won't need it, will you?"

Ashworth conceded that point with a slight shrug. Opening his coat, he drew out the pistol and handed it to Archie.

Archie shoved it under his belt on his left side. He carried Cap's revolver on his right side. Waving the rifle at Cap now, he motioned for him to leave the cave.

Cap hesitated. He looked at Jane and saw her nod. She put up a brave front, but her eyes revealed fear.

He turned to Ashworth. "I'll give you half an hour. If you haven't started down the mountain by then, I'll come back. . . ."

"McKenna, that is quite enough!" Ashworth snapped.

With a last look at Jane and Jamie, Cap turned and left the cave.

He led the way down the rocky mountainside to the knee-high grass of the valley floor. Following the game trail there, he waded the creek and returned to the meadow where the horses grazed. Archie and Leonard had dropped back, following at a distance.

Cap knelt and drank from the creek. When the gunmen entered the meadow, he stood.

"Hand over my Colt," he said to Archie.

Archie answered with a shake of his head. While walking, he had carried his repeater over his shoulder. Now he brought it to bear on Cap.

Leonard stepped closer. "We got us some unfinished business, don't we?"

Cap eyed them. "What have you gents talked yourselves into?"

Leonard set his rifle down in the grass. "Time to even the score for dumping me outa the saddle."

Cap watched him draw the Bowie knife from the sheath on his belt. "You aim to cut me for that?" he asked.

Leonard glanced at Archie. "See? I told you this cow

chaser ain't all the way stupid."

Cap took his hat off and flung it aside. He watched the smaller man crouch and slowly advance, thrusting the polished blade out in front of him as he closed the distance.

"Give me a fair fight," Cap said.

Leonard paused. "You carry a knife?"

Cap shook his head.

"Too bad," Leonard said, and advanced another step. "Then it won't be fair, I guess."

Archie laughed shrilly. "Don't kill him, Lenny. Cut him . . . just cut him some."

Cap raised his fists, backing away.

"Run," Leonard taunted, "and Archie'll wing you. You got a choice . . . a couple cuts, or a bullet-smashed leg."

Cap moved to his right, eyes fixed on Leonard. At first, he considered finding out if Archie was a better shot than he had demonstrated when he fired at White Moon Woman. He could run — or take on little Leonard with his big blade. The moment of indecision passed, when Leonard took two quick steps and lunged.

Cap darted to his left. The knife blade flashed by, wide of the mark by inches. The instant that Leonard halted and tried to turn back, Cap moved on him. He drew back his fist and threw a quick punch. He hit Leonard in the temple, not hard, but with enough force to stagger the man. Cap watched him catch his balance, pause, and then come after him again, eyes blinking now.

Cap backed away. He feinted to his left and side-stepped to the right, a motion that rarely failed to haze a horse into a stall. The move worked on Leonard, too, and, when the man was momentarily frozen in mid-step, Cap set his feet and cocked his fist. He let go again, this time catching him squarely on the chin. Leonard's eyes rolled, and his knees buckled.

Cap drew back his fist, but, before he could hit Leonard again, he heard a curse. Too late he glimpsed Archie swinging the Winchester.

The barrel of the repeater struck the back of his head, hard, like a soundless explosion. The fragrant green grass at his feet seemed to rush up, and then Cap rolled over in it, looking skyward. In his dizzying vision he saw Archie looming over him. Then Leonard came into view, his scowling, beard-stubbled face framed by blue sky. The knife blade glinted as he raised it for a downward thrust.

A rifle shot halted Leonard's arm in mid-air. Cap heard a man's deep voice call out, ordering the pair to drop their weapons. When they hesitated, a second shot rang out from the forest shadows.

"The next one won't be over your heads!" warned a voice.

Archie dropped his rifle. Leonard flung the knife away and raised his arms straight up.

Cap tried to sit, but fell back. He held his head in an effort to stop the dizzying motion of the earth. Rolling to his side, his eyes slowly focused on a movement near the treeline. Joshua Potter strode toward him, Spencer held barrel high. Then came darkness.

Cap sensed someone nearby, but the deep voice calling to him seemed to come from afar.

"Cap . . . Cap . . . you hurt bad?"

He opened his eyes, trying to focus on the shadowy form against the evening sky. He shook his head, but could not make any words come out of his mouth.

"Never liked the looks of them fellers," Potter said. "I seen you in the meadow, here, just as that one clubbed you. Figured I'd better even up the odds."

"Tha . . . tha . . . thanks," Cap said hoarsely.

"Take it easy," Potter said. "A whack to the haid ties a man's tongue fer a spell."

Cap sat up slowly, struggling for consciousness as though coming awake after a deep sleep.

"You've been out cold an hour or more," Potter added.

Cap looked around. He saw the gunmen, now bound hand and foot, lying in the meadow fifty yards away. He struggled to stand. With Potter's help he came upright and quickly discovered his knees would not hold him. Leaning on the big man, he made his way to the creek. Cap dropped down at the bank and splashed water on his face. The cold water numbed his skin. His head started to clear.

"Got to . . . got to. . . ." Cap heard himself stammering. He knew the words he wanted to say, but could not get his tongue around them.

"Take it easy," Potter said again.

"Got to . . . go . . . cave."

"Wait till you get your feet under you, suh."

Cap drank. Then he splashed more glacier-cold water on his face. His head throbbed, but he managed to stand on his own. The dizziness abated. He left the creek with Potter close at his side.

After searching in the grass, he found his Colt where Archie had dropped it. He picked it up and checked the barrel for débris and the cylinder for loads, and then holstered it. He felt undressed without his hat, but, when he picked it up off the ground and put it on, pain stabbed at the back of his head. He took it off and tossed it by his saddle.

Potter pointed across the creek. "Looks like you won't have to make that hike, suh."

Cap turned. Jane and Jamie, rucksacks on their backs, were walking along the game trail, heads bowed. They were followed by Ashworth. The three forded the creek. When

Jane drew closer, Cap saw a smudge of campfire soot on the side of her face. Jamie walked close to her, his hand in hers.

Now Ashworth jogged ahead, an expression of alarm on his face. His gaze shifted from Cap and Potter to the bound men in the grass.

"What the hell's going on here?" he demanded. "What do you think you're doing?"

It was Potter who responded. "Your men was fixing to cut Cap." He held up the Bowie knife. "So I disarmed 'em."

"You listen to me!" Ashworth shouted as he whirled to face Potter. "Put that knife down. . . ."

"Ashworth," Cap broke in, "you're not giving orders, now. You're taking them."

"What . . . ?" he began.

Cap gestured to the gunmen. "Go join your friends, while we get things cleared up."

"Cleared up?" Ashworth demanded. His voice faltered. "McKenna, I don't know what happened between you and these two men, but they had no orders from me to harm you. . . ."

Cap repeated: "Go over there and sit down."

Ashworth made no move to obey, until Cap took a step toward him. Then the lawyer turned and strode angrily to the center of the meadow. Arms folded across his chest, he stood by the gunmen, but did not sit down.

Cap's gaze shifted to Jane and Jamie. He moved closer to them. "Jane."

She lifted her head. The smear of soot almost covered the dark bruise on her cheek.

"Jane, did he hit you?"

In a low voice she replied: "I've decided . . . to return to Chicago . . . with Mister Ashworth."

"He hit you, didn't he?"

She shook her head.

"Jane," Cap said.

"He hit her!" Jamie blurted. "He said savages in these mountains will kill us . . . he said we'll die, if we don't go back to Chicago with him! Cap, we don't want to go. . . ."

Jane reached out and put her hand on her brother's shoulder. *"Shhhh,"* she said.

"Ashworth won't hurt you," Cap said. "I promise you."

Anger made his head throb. He turned and strode over to Ashworth and his hired men.

"First thing in the morning, gents," he said, "I'll guide you out of here and point you toward Denver. Head for Chicago, and don't come back."

"McKenna, I advise you not to interfere," Ashworth said. "The girl's headstrong. You don't know the pertinent facts. . . ."

Cap grasped the lapel of his coat. "Mister, I know all I need to know."

"You're a damned fool," Ashworth whispered.

"Take a swing at me . . . or do you only punch women?"

Ashworth's face darkened.

"Sit down," Cap said, shoving him, "before I knock you down."

Ashworth yielded. He slumped in the grass a dozen yards from Archie and Leonard. Amid his threats and curses, Cap bound him with a rope.

Cap indicated to Potter, who was now with Jane and Jamie, that he wanted to talk to him and took him aside.

"I may have bitten off more than I can chew. I need some help."

"Name it," Potter said.

He jerked his head toward the three men. "Come daybreak,

98

I'll march them out of here and send them on their way. But it'll take two of us to get through the night."

"Yes, suh. What shift you want me to take?"

"First half of the night," Cap replied. "After I get some rest, maybe my head won't hurt as much."

Potter nodded. "I'll hike back to my camp and let White Moon Woman know where I am."

Jane and Jamie gathered a pile of twigs and dried branches while Cap built a campfire near the creek. When the flames were up, he added some pine boughs. The thick smoke drove away the mosquitoes and deerflies. The group settled around the fire.

Drowsy, Cap leaned back on his elbows. His head ached, but, at least, the throbbing pain was gone.

Jane sat on a saddle blanket Cap had spread out on the grass. Settling in after a meal from tins, she managed a weak smile when their eyes met over the leaping flames.

"I owe you an explanation," she said. "And an apology. I should have told you. . . ."

"Told me what?" Cap asked.

"The truth," she said. "All of it. Jamie and I came here to escape, to get away from Mister Ashworth. He locked us in our house and threatened to kill us. I should have told you." Her voice trailed off. After a long moment, she went on: "I hoped he wouldn't find us . . . I just did not think he would pursue us all the way out here."

"He has no right to hurt you or threaten you," Cap said. "I'll run him out of here. After daybreak, move your camp. You'll be safe."

Jamie agreed and spoke with enthusiasm. "Don't worry, Sis. We can hide as long as we want!"

She cast a doubtful look his way and then hugged him. "Until we run out of food." Jane looked skyward. "I thought we could escape in this wilderness . . . like Daddy's spirit escaping to heaven. Now . . . now, I don't know."

After dark Potter returned. White Moon Woman came with him, carrying their baby. They appeared out of the starlit night, silently stepping into the edge of the fire glow. Jane gasped, startled until she recognized Potter.

Cap introduced her to White Moon Woman. He grinned as Jane moved closer to her and admired the baby. She uttered soft sounds, gently touching his cheek. The two women looked at one another in the firelight and smiled in feminine communication that needed no words.

"Camp with us a spell," Potter said to Jane and Jamie, "and you'll learn from White Moon Woman how to live in these mountain valleys. Rabbit or root vegetable, there's plenty of food here, if you know where to find it and how to get at it."

Cap saw Jane smile at Jamie's excited reply. "See! I told you! We can stay here as long as we need to!"

"McKenna!" Ashworth shouted. "McKenna!"

Cap left the fire. He walked to the center of the meadow where he saw the three starlit forms.

"McKenna," Ashworth said, "come to your senses, man. I assure you, you don't fully comprehend what you're getting into. . . ."

"Then tell me," Cap broke in. "In plain English."

Ashworth was silent for a long moment. "All right . . . but alone."

Against his better judgment, Cap freed Ashworth and took him across the meadow near the trees. At forest's edge they halted, facing one another in the pine-scented darkness.

"The future of Reynolds Overland is at stake."

"You already told me that much."

Ashworth paused. "I assure you, everyone's best interests will be served. . . ."

"Stop assuring me," Cap broke in, "and tell me what the hell's going on."

Ashworth drew a deep breath. "As heir to Reynolds Overland, Jane holds the majority share of the company. It's held in a trust administered by a judge. She can sell, but she refuses."

"You're the Reynolds' lawyer," Cap said. "Why don't you go along with her wishes?"

"I own one-fourth of Reynolds Overland," Ashworth explained. "J. Stuart Reynolds had a reputation as a shrewd businessman, but he was reckless . . . a damned fool. Without me, Reynolds Overland would not exist today. Reynolds went broke before he came to Chicago. Two years ago he got overextended again. My cash and my advice kept Reynolds Overland rolling. All I ask is the opportunity to buy out Jane's share. She's child-like. She simply does not comprehend the realities of the business world. . . ."

"Hold on," Cap said. "Are you saying Reynolds Overland is going broke?"

Ashworth made no reply.

"This is like pulling teeth," Cap said. "Lay it all out."

"It's not public knowledge. You must swear. . . ."

"This isn't a courtroom," Cap said. "I'm not swearing to anything."

After a long silence, Ashworth replied in a whisper: "The Union Pacific plans to run a spur to Denver. It's been rumored for a long time, but I know work will start soon. After completion, freight will be shipped by rail. Reynolds Overland cannot compete with rail cars." He took a sharp breath. "Don't you see? The company must be sold before word gets out. It's the only way we can avoid losing everything."

"Jane knows this?" Cap asked.

He nodded. "She thinks Reynolds Overland can operate

at a smaller profit, and all the men can keep their jobs. She's naïve. . . ."

"But if she owns three-fourths of the company," Cap said, "she has a right to make up her own mind."

Ashworth demanded in a loud whisper: "Don't you understand? She'll take me down with her . . . a mere child!"

"A child who won't obey you," Cap said. "So you hit her."

"I lost patience," he said, exasperated. "The girl's as bull-headed as her father was. With so much at stake, you'd have done the same if you were in my place."

Cap shook his head. "That's where you're wrong, Ashworth."

Chapter Ten

Reminding him of bunch quitters ready to bolt, Cap herded the reluctant city men through the mountains toward his homestead. He had disarmed them. As a further precaution, he had taken the boots of all three and tied them behind his saddle.

As wartime experience with prisoners had taught him, a man without footgear was at a severe disadvantage. He hoped this trio in only socked feet would be less likely to hatch a scheme to overwhelm him somewhere along the trail.

At first light he had left the camp in the meadow. He had bid good bye to Jane and Jamie, White Moon Woman, and then he had thanked Potter. The man had stood guard all night. Cap had awoken with an aching head, but felt refreshed.

He had left the two Winchesters and ammunition with Potter and Jamie, and had tossed Ashworth's handgun into his saddlebag. He had given the Bowie knife to White Moon Woman.

He was not a man to run horses into the ground under any circumstances, but on this day he was eager to get back to his homestead. Through the morning and early afternoon he pressed the livery horses and their riders as hard as he dared. Switchbacking up and down forested ridges and riding through grassy valleys, he continued eastward toward the prairie, resting man and beast in brief stops along the way.

The sun cast long shadows through the pines when they topped the last ridge overlooking his homestead. Cap held a tight rein. The buckskin had caught sight or scent of the barn and tossed his head in his wish to be in his stall.

Ashworth and the two hired men grimaced, miserable from a long day on horseback, their feet rubbed raw by the stirrups. Cap saw them grasp the saddle horns, holding on for dear life as their mounts staggered down the last slope.

Near the bottom of the ridge he looked ahead. Movement at the cabin caught his eye as a figure edged back from a corner of the building. He had company. The view from the bench told him no freight outfit was there.

Drawing his revolver, Cap let the gelding have his head, and passed the three men at a fast canter. As he closed the distance, a stocky figure stepped into the open — a youth wearing overalls and a farmer's high-crowned straw hat.

Cap holstered his gun and hauled back on the reins.

"Evening, Mister McKenna."

"Evening, Hezekiah."

Cap dismounted, but, before he could speak, the young man announced his chore list. He had mucked the stalls in the barn, cleaned out the corral, fed and tended the horses, and lugged water from the creek. He had even cleaned ashes from the wood stove and swept out the dirt floor of the cabin.

"Much obliged," Cap said in surprise. He glanced over his shoulder. Ashworth and his hired men were riding slowly past the aspen grove, heading toward Trapper Creek.

"I'm on my own now. . . ."

Cap interrupted him. "We'll talk later."

Hezekiah looked past him. "Hey, I've seen them three citified horsebackers. They stopped by our . . . by Pa's farm, asking directions. Hey, they're riding without boots. What for?"

"I'll tell you later."

Hezekiah reached for the buckskin's reins. "Want me to feed him and rub him down?"

Cap nodded. He untied the boots and carried them to Trapper Creek as Hezekiah led the gelding away. Ashworth and his hired men sat on the bank, their bare feet submerged in the water.

Cap dropped their boots to the ground. With a glance over their shoulders at the sound of the boots hitting ground, Archie and Leonard both cursed him.

"You gents mind your manners," Cap said, "and I'll rustle up a hot meal before I send you on your way."

Ashworth turned abruptly, grabbing his boots. "I won't stay here a minute longer than I have to."

"Remember that, if you get a notion to ride back this way," Cap said, and walked away.

In the barn he filled three nosebags with oats. He walked back to Trapper Creek and put them on the livery horses.

"No need for the critters to suffer," he said.

Ashworth ignored him.

Again, Cap returned to the barn. After helping Hezekiah tend the buckskin, the two went to the cabin, carrying the saddlebags and rifle. Cap hung his belt and holstered Colt on a peg by the door. Meanwhile, Hezekiah stoked a fire in the stove, intermittently watching Ashworth from the doorway.

The city men stayed long enough to grain their horses, eat a meal of canned food, and fill their canteens. Then they tightened cinches, swung up, and rode away without looking back.

During supper, Cap answered Hezekiah's questions, telling him who the riders were and why they had come. He poured a shot of rye whiskey into his last cup of coffee. Then he looked across the rough pine table at his guest.

"Your father know you're here?"

Hezekiah shook his head.

"What happened?"

"Pa said iffen I don't obey him and take his authority as pure as God's law, then I ain't worthy to be his son. Well, I told him he warn't worthy to be my pa. Packed my clothes and left in the night."

"Your ma know?"

"Told her I was leaving, but I didn't say where." He leaned forward. "Mister McKenna, I can learn the cattle-raising business. I'm a hard worker. Like I told you, I'll do any chore around this place. I can learn from you, and someday I'll prove up my own homestead land."

Cap exhaled. He craved sleep. "We'll talk it through in the morning."

"I'll take that 'ere bunk in the barn," Hezekiah said, standing.

By lamplight, Cap watched him move to the doorway. For a reason beyond his ken, he recalled youthful faces from the past — faces of cavalrymen who had served in Company B.

"Hezekiah."

He turned. "Yes, sir?"

"First, call me Cap."

"Yes, sir . . . I mean, Cap."

Cap stood. He crossed the room to his bunk and opened his saddlebags. Lifting out the pistol he had taken from Ashworth, he handed it to him. "Know how to use this?"

Wide-eyed, Hezekiah nodded. "Pa, he's got a revolver. I've fired it."

"This one's yours," Cap said.

"Are you . . . you sure you want to give it me?"

Cap nodded.

"Well, thank you!" he said excitedly. He turned the short-barreled six-shooter over in his hand. "Thank you very much, sir . . . Cap! Thank you!"

"I don't expect those city men to come back tonight," Cap

106

said, "but, if you hear horsemen or see anything, fire off a shot."

At first light Cap built a fire in the stove and put water on for coffee. Pulling on his boots, he stepped out of the cabin. As was his habit from the first day he built this place, he surveyed the land before him. The expanse of prairie, stretching out from the base of the foothills, was gray-brown from the grass fire, not the pitch black he had seen the morning after the blaze.

"Morning, Cap."

Startled, he turned and saw Hezekiah sitting on the ground at the corner of the cabin, gun in hand. The youth scrambled to his feet.

"No one came around here," Hezekiah said. "Stayed awake most of the night. I'd have knowed if anyone skulked about."

Cap nodded approval. "You're a good man, Hezekiah."

Following Cap's gaze, he looked at a reddening sky over the horizon for several minutes. When he spoke, his voice was subdued, as though talking to himself. "Pa, he never told me I done good. He always told me to work harder. Pray to God and work harder, he always said." He paused. "How kin you work harder when you already done your best?"

Over the next three days Hezekiah tackled chores from sawing and splitting firewood to carrying water and helping with the cooking and cleaning. He did not have to be told anything more than once, and quickly took on tasks on his own. He observed Cap working with the draft horses, and stood by when a Reynolds teamster rolled up to the barn, ready to lend a hand when Cap gave the word.

At noon of the fourth day Cap spotted the rider, at first little more than a speck on the prairie. The rider drew closer, head bowed, as though crossing hell's floor. Mounted on a splotched gray mule, the large, thick-bodied figure wore tattered overalls and a straw hat. Half a dozen goats ran loose before him. Cap discerned who was coming long before he made out the features in the broad, sun-browned face.

"Hezekiah."

The young man had been forking hay in the barn, and now he stepped outside. He gazed out toward the prairie.

"I dreamed Pa came huntin' fer me," Hezekiah said, coming to Cap's side. "Dreamed he whupped me. . . ."

Cap turned to him. "What do you aim to do?"

"Stop him from whuppin' me," he replied, and managed a grin.

Cap took the pitchfork from his hands. "I'll let you two work it out," he said, and strode to the barn.

He watched from the shadows of the runway as Ezekiel Haynes forded Trapper Creek and rode straight up to Hezekiah. The goats stayed behind at the water's edge.

Haynes halted. Father and son gazed at one another in silence, until Haynes swung a leg over the mule's neck. He slid heavily to the ground.

Cap saw them move closer together. Their voices rose, but he could not make out their words. Then he saw Hezekiah's body stiffen.

The youth shook his head in a gesture of defiance. His father swiftly drew back his arm. Before he could backhand Hezekiah, he was punched in the face. His head snapped back, his arms dropping to his sides.

Cap watched Hezekiah stand his ground, fists up, expression determined. Bright red blood trickled from Haynes's cut lip. The farmer stood still, as though rooted. He heard Haynes's commanding voice, and in the next instant Hezekiah punched him in the face again. This time Haynes staggered back.

Cap knew Hezekiah made a mistake when he did not press his advantage. He must have believed his father was hurt, for he lowered his arms, open-handed, in a gesture of sympathy. Haynes lashed out. He slapped his son and then grabbed him like a bear. He drove him to the ground, kneeing him in the crotch as dust lifted around them.

Hezekiah moaned, but showed his strength by digging in with booted feet and rolling to his side. One short, powerful punch to his father's gut, and he freed himself. Coming up to his knees, Hezekiah raised his right fist and slugged his prone father — once, twice, then repeatedly in piston-like punches to the face.

Cap dropped the pitchfork. He sprinted out of the barn, aware of Hezekiah's sobs as he pummeled his father. Then Cap was on top of the two, and he grabbed Hezekiah's forearm.

"That's enough! Enough!"

Knuckles bloodied and his face wet with tears and sweat, Hezekiah looked at Cap as though not recognizing him for a moment. Then his arm went slack. Cap let go. The youth coughed. He gasped for breath.

Cap raised up and went for a bucket from the trough. He sloshed water on Haynes's battered face and stepped back when the man revived and sat upright. Haynes looked around, as though getting his bearings. Eyes startled, he gingerly touched his jaw and upper lip. He examined his bloody fingertips as though they were foreign objects. Without a word, he stood. His head bowed, he slowly walked to the gray mule and gathered the reins. He grasped a handful of mane and with great effort pulled himself up onto the mule's back.

"Pa."

Haynes turned the big animal and rode out of the yard. The goats fled in various directions when he crossed Trapper Creek.

Cap saw a pained expression knit Hezekiah's brow as he watched his father ride across the burned prairie. Setting the bucket down, he reached out and placed his hand on the youth's shoulder.

That evening Hezekiah told Cap that his father knew where to find him because the three city men had stopped at the farm on their way to Denver. They had described a husky young man in overalls and battered straw hat at Cap McKenna's homestead.

"Looks like he didn't want the goats," Cap said.

"Pa went into a rage when he found out you sent them," Hezekiah said. "Said he wouldn't take charity, not from nobody, 'specially not from the dark angel."

They were both quiet for a long time, then Hezekiah explained: "Pa, he wants me and my brothers to claim homestead land next to his farm when we come of age. Cap, I don't want to spend my life behind a plow."

A week passed with no sign of Ashworth, and Cap figured the man had left the territory. He discovered that was wishful thinking the day he spotted dust billowing over the prairie. Dark shapes in the distance gradually defined themselves as horses and riders in two long lines. The sound of the hoofbeats drifted through the air like a muted drum roll.

Cap moved to the corral. Hezekiah joined him there. The youth sat on the top pole, looking at Cap with an unspoken question.

"Fifty, sixty troopers," Cap said. "Moving fast."

Half a dozen advance riders galloped ahead of the formation. Scouts, Cap saw now, led by Major Symington. Minutes later he recognized Colonel Tom Sully at the head of the column. A civilian rode at his side — Stanley Ashworth.

Chapter Eleven

Cap greeted Major Luke Symington, after he had splashed across the creek and reined to a halt near the corral. Hezekiah watched intently.

Symington replied with a formal — "Good afternoon, Mister McKenna." — and raised a gloved hand to the brim of his campaign hat.

He made no move to dismount. Cap saw the advance riders fan out behind him, carbines at the ready as the eyes of each black trooper were fixed on him. The men were clearly under orders to take control here and await the arrival of their commanding officer.

The main column halted at the far bank of Trapper Creek. Colonel Tom Sully forded it alone, leaving Ashworth behind.

"Mister McKenna!" Sully called out, reining up beside Symington. He dismounted and came forward, methodically pulling off his cuffed gloves.

"Colonel," Cap greeted him. He thrust out his hand to shake, but withdrew it when Sully did not reciprocate.

"I suppose you know why I'm here," he said, the brim of his campaign hat shading his pale blue eyes.

Cap gestured toward Ashworth. "He's the reason. Get that man off my land."

"I've heard Mister Ashworth's side of the story," Sully said. "Now I want to hear yours."

"Get him off my land," Cap repeated.

"Mister Ashworth is in my custody," Sully said. He pushed

111

his hat back and dragged a hand down his jaw. "The man is prepared to lodge charges against you for deadly assault, Mister McKenna. Now is your time to speak."

Cap relented. He gave him a shortened account of the events since Ashworth first rode into his yard with the pair of hired gunmen. He described meeting Jane and Jamie Reynolds, and concluded by informing Sully that as heirs to the Reynolds' estate, the sister and brother wanted no part of Stanley Ashworth. Back in Chicago the lawyer had threatened them, and they had fled.

"When he caught up with them," Cap concluded, "he bullied them, and struck Miss Reynolds across the face."

Colonel Sully considered this account, a version undoubtedly at odds with the one he had heard from Ashworth. "Seems to me you're leaving out the most important element."

"Sir?" Cap asked.

"Your explanation conveniently ignores the participation of Sergeant Joshua Potter," Sully said. "Fits the pattern, doesn't it?"

"What pattern?"

"You always deny involvement," he said. "When you lured Sergeant Potter out of my field camp, you claimed innocence then, too. Now you're weaving a similar tale."

"Colonel Sully, I am telling you the truth."

"The entire truth?" Sully demanded. "Mister Ashworth tells me Potter threatened to kill him and fired on the two men in his employ."

"And saved my life," Cap said. "One of his men came at me with a knife, while the other trained his rifle on me. Did he mention that?"

Sully shook his head.

"Potter had nothing to do with Ashworth's plan to kidnap Jane and Jamie," Cap said.

"You make serious allegations," Sully said. "You may be telling the truth . . . or part of it. I will grant you that much. I can establish the whole truth by interviewing Miss Reynolds and her brother, can't I?"

Cap nodded.

"I assume you know where they are," Sully said. "And I assume you know where Sergeant Potter is camped."

Cap did not reply.

"Is Potter with the Indian woman?" Sully asked. "Has he taken up with a tribe of savages?"

Cap answered the last question. "I haven't seen a band of Indians."

Sully studied him. "Take me to his camp."

"You gave the man a lashing on account of me," Cap said. "I won't be a party to that again."

"With or without your help, I will find him," Sully said. "Just as I will locate Miss Reynolds and her brother."

"You don't need me," Cap said. "You've got Ashworth."

"You know better than that," Sully replied. "When Mister Ashworth arrived in my camp, he could barely sit a saddle. He left his two associates in the Denver House, both of them stove up from their ordeal. He's determined to speak to Miss Reynolds, and I offered to aid in his search. You know the back country, McKenna. You will save us all a great deal of time by guiding my troopers through passable routes."

When Cap did not reply, Sully continued: "Your full co-operation will prove to me that you are innocent of aiding and abetting an A. W. O. L. sergeant in possession of government property. In exchange for your services, no charges will be filed against you . . . by me or by Ashworth."

"Colonel, you're judge and jury?" Cap asked.

He gripped his gloves and slapped them into the palm of his hand. "I hereby order you to serve as guide. . . ."

"Colonel, I'm a civilian," Cap broke in. "You can't order me to do anything."

"You are a civilian in a territory of the United States," Sully said, and moved a step closer. "As a commanding officer on the frontier, I am empowered by the federal government to enforce the law. Disobey, Mister McKenna, and I'll have you shackled and escorted to Denver."

Cap met Sully's blue-eyed gaze. Behind him on horseback, Symington looked on impassively. Cap recalled an earlier comment from the major — a warning that Sully was quick to punish. Cap drew a deep breath. Standing up to the colonel would only force his hand. After a long moment, he turned and saw Hezekiah staring at him, wide-eyed.

"Looks like I need your help. Can you tend the horses for a couple days?"

"Yes, sir!" Hezekiah replied, jumping down and standing stiffly as though called to attention.

Cap turned to Sully. "I'll ride with you . . . on one condition."

"I'm not here to negotiate, McKenna," Sully said impatiently. But he blinked and sighed. "Well, what is it?"

"Ashworth," Cap replied. "Keep him out of my path." Then he turned and headed for the barn.

Cap rode up the ridge beyond his homestead, leading Major Symington and his party of advance riders. A long line of paired troopers stretched out behind them. Scouts flanked the column left and right.

Through the afternoon progress was slow. Loaded down with bedrolls lashed behind their saddles, the men in blue carried haversacks, nose bags and pouches of oats, canteens, trenching tools, and carbines and revolvers with extra bandoleers of ammunition. Cavalry mounts were strong, but not fast.

The main column was led by Colonel Tom Sully. Two captains followed. Behind them rode Ashworth with a troop sergeant. Pack mules and spare mounts brought up the rear. The formation was cumbersome in the forested, uneven terrain.

Cap thought back to the war, remembering the slow movement of infantry and even mounted battalions. He had often wished soldiers traveled faster, lessening the enemy's time to fortify. This strategy employed by Sully today was effective in protecting the main column against ambush from a strong enemy force. But no such force was here.

Cap urged his gelding ahead. He had made his decision the moment he agreed to Sully's order. He had no intention of leading him to Potter's camp. The sooner he got this over with, the better.

Sully had been right about one thing. Cap knew this country better than any trooper, including Symington and the men who had barged through here in their first search for Joshua Potter. Even with the slow-moving column this afternoon, he covered more ground in half a day than he would have thought possible. With the sun slipping behind the great mountain peak to the west, Cap led the way up a rocky ridge. On the other side, he remembered a grassy bowl ringed by pine trees.

"Meadow over yonder," Cap said, turning in the saddle as he spoke to Symington. "Plenty of water and grass."

"Lead the way," the major replied. "We'll camp there, if it's suitable."

Cap topped the ridge and made his way down the other side through the heavy timber. Fifty yards downslope he broke out of the forest. Thick-trunked spruce and tall pine trees ringed a large meadow. Lush foliage was sprinkled with wildflowers blooming like gems in vivid reds, blues, and yellows. A small creek coursed through the far edge of the meadow.

Cap reined up and dismounted. The major halted at his side. He surveyed this place, while the troopers gathered behind him. Nodding his approval, Symington turned and dispatched one man to pass the order back to Sully.

The major leaned close to Cap and spoke in a low voice: "I know you resent Sully. You're not alone." He glanced back to make certain the troopers were out of earshot. "But, if you have concocted some scheme to lead us on a phantom chase, I suggest you abandon it. The colonel can make life more miserable for you than he already has."

Cap looked at him questioningly.

"You may not be aware of it," Symington went on, "but he has the power to revoke your homestead papers."

Cap watched as Symington left the advance group and approached Sully and the main column. Pondering Symington's warning, he led his horse across the width of the meadow and forded the creek. He found a level spot between the grassy bank and the edge of the forest and stripped the gelding and began to make camp.

Presently Colonel Sully led his column out of the trees. Symington had met him. The two officers conferred and rode up a knoll across the way. At the crest they dismounted.

Cap pulled off his boots. He rolled a smoke and reclined on an elbow as bellowed commands were repeated through the ranks. The sight and sound of soldiers making camp sparked memories, taking his mind back to the time when he wore a uniform.

The knoll was an elevated position, a natural place of command. Sully kept his officers and enlisted men busy with the details of making camp and posting sentries. Ashworth sat in the grass there, too, at times staring across the meadow at Cap.

Major Symington left his superior officer's side, issuing orders to a captain who in turn passed them along to the lieu-tenants. Like worker bees, the lieutenants moved between the knoll and the campsite, repeating instructions to ranking ser-geants who barked them out to corporals. Weapons were stacked, horses hobbled, and firewood gathered from forest deadfalls. Soon smoky campfires blazed.

Reconnaissance scouts rode out in pairs to search for sign of Indians. Cap had overheard enough talk through the after-noon to know that Sully was uneasy about confronting war-riors. The possibility of ambush, Cap figured, was the reason for the cumbersome formation today.

Sentries were posted. One stood among the tree shadows behind Cap. Standing, Cap walked in his socked feet into the forest in search of firewood. While gathering twigs and dead branches, he noted the distance between this sentry and the next one.

No tents were erected. Cap knew what that meant. This was a field camp. It would be struck at dawn when the march resumed. All the men, even officers, would sleep under the stars tonight, ready to move out with a minimum of delay.

Content to be alone, Cap built a fire. He crushed roasted beans with his gun butt and made coffee, then banked the glowing red coals to heat several tins of food. After eating leisurely, he washed his gear.

At dusk Cap saw Symington headed his way. The tall of-ficer strode through the camp, crossing the creek to Cap's fire. He pulled off his campaign hat and ran a hand through short-cropped blond hair. Then he knelt.

"Coffee?"

Symington shook his head. "I'll get straight to the point." The major fell silent, clearly uncomfortable.

Amused, Cap watched the firelight play across his angular face.

"Tom wants you to know you're within the perimeter of our camp. You will be challenged should you wander."

Cap grinned. "You mean, he doesn't want me running off."

Symington nodded.

"Tell your colonel he can go to hell."

"Can't do that," Symington replied, deadpan. "This is a serious matter. Tom said to remind you we are in hostile territory. Sentries have orders to shoot on sight." With one last meaningful look, the major stood. He turned and walked away, his riding boots splashing through the shallow creek.

Cap spread his blanket in the grass. He lay back, his head on his saddle. The murmurs of the retiring troopers and the sounds of penned horses brought more memories cascading into his mind. He closed his eyes, dozing until he heard the sound of water splashing, punctuated by an urgent whisper.

He sat up. In the starlit darkness four shadows swiftly closed in — four men, hatless, bent low — dropping to their knees at Cap's side. One spoke in a low tone.

"Mistah McKenna, suh, maybe you 'member me. I was pullin' sentry duty the evenin' you rode into our camp outside Denver."

"I remember you."

"Folks call me Marcus," he said.

"Howdy, Marcus. I'm Cap."

"Well, uh, we got us a matter fer pondering . . . Cap."

"What is it?"

"Well, suh, a bunch of us in our platoon, we was talking and . . . well, rumors, they's flying like bats at midnight, and we was a-wondering . . . well, suh, we served with Joshua, and we was just a-wondering if he's living with Indians."

Another trooper whispered: "Suh, some soldiers claim we's a-gonna fight Cheyennes 'cause ol' Josh, he done put one over

118

on the colonel, and Sully, he's out fer almighty revenge."

The men were almost faceless in the dark, yet Cap felt the intensity of their gazes.

"If Colonel Sully aims to fight Cheyennes," Cap said, "he'll need eyes sharper than mine."

"You ain't guiding us to a Cheyenne camp?" Marcus asked.

"No," Cap said.

"Then where are we headed?"

"The colonel claims he wants to interview a young woman and her brother, Jane and Jamie Reynolds. But it's Potter he's after. Sully guessed right when he figured the Reynolds are camped with him."

"You done seen Josh?" Marcus asked.

"How's the ol' sarge doing?" queried another trooper.

"He plans to winter in these mountains," Cap said. "So he and White Moon Woman can raise their boy and live in peace. That's what he told me."

"Well, thank you, suh, for clearin' this matter up," Marcus said. "We figured we was gonna have to fight Indians and ol' Josh, too, and in this here mountain country with all these trees and rocks fer hidin' places, well, suh, not a man here is willin' to die for the sake of Sully's revenge."

"An' we sure as hell don't want to be shooting at ol' Josh," said another trooper.

"Or him shooting back at us," said Marcus, and the others chuckled.

"Good night, suh . . . and thanks."

The men moved away, abruptly stopping when Cap said: "Wait."

"Suh?" Marcus whispered as he came back.

"That sentry posted behind us," he said, "might see a man leading his horse into the trees tonight."

"You fixin' to bust camp?" Marcus whispered.

"I aim to resolve this thing and help out Potter at the same time," Cap said. "And I don't want to take a bullet on my way out."

"Suh, he won't shoot you. We'll see to it."

"I don't want to make trouble for you or the sentry," Cap said. "Because of me, Potter got a lashing. So did a sentry."

"Don't fret," Marcus said. "We bust camp all the time . . . Denver, Laramie, Santa Fé, any town where we can get a drink and a woman. Hardly ever get caught."

"Yes, suh," added another trooper. "We'll fix it."

Chapter Twelve

At first light Cap touched his heels to the buckskin, increasing the pace. Until now he had traveled in near darkness with a loose rein in a westward direction, alternately guiding and then allowing the sure-footed animal to find passage through the black-timbered forests and over ridges bathed in starlight.

Cap had departed Sully's encampment without incident. After midnight he had pulled on his boots, quietly saddled his horse, and led him out of the meadow into the pines, unchallenged. He was grateful to Marcus. A nervous sentry standing guard in Indian country at night would have blazed away at any sound or shadow had he not been tipped off.

Sunrise found Cap making his way downslope through the lodgepole forest. With the familiar roar of the waterfall in his ears and mist on his face, he took off his hat and wiped his brow on a shirt sleeve. A break in the trees showed the cascading water far below. Downstream beaver ponds mirrored the sunlit sky of morning. Cap put his hat back on. Tugging the brim brought a grimace. The back of his head still hurt, swollen where the rifle barrel had struck him.

Reaching the bottom, he guided his horse into the meadow of high grass where teepee rings marked the abandoned Indian campsite. He rode past the charred remains of his old campfire. Beyond the chain of beaver ponds and surrounding marsh, the forest of towering ponderosas closed in. Riding close to the creekbank, he dismounted and studied the soft ground for sign. He saw animal tracks, but no imprints left by shod horses or booted humans.

Cap looked around for other clues, but saw only a forest floor littered with pine cones, dried needles, and tangles of fallen branches. Potter's camp was around here somewhere, he figured, and moved on into the forest. For long minutes he searched, knowing time was slipping away. Undoubtedly Sully had discovered his escape at dawn and dispatched a squad of his best trackers to give chase. Even with a head start of several hours, cavalrymen riding in full daylight would close the distance.

Cap knew he had to take a chance. Drawing his revolver, he thumbed back the hammer and aimed skyward. He squeezed the trigger. Powder smoke drifted in among the pine boughs. He holstered the revolver. Pulling the makings out of his shirt pocket, he rolled a smoke and knelt by the stream that wound through the forest.

He smoked half the cigarette and then stood up. In a pool of clear water, trout darted away from his shadow. As Cap dropped the cigarette and ground it out, bluejays called from the high treetops. Causing a sudden rustle of twigs, a pair of black-tailed squirrels bounded through the pines, chattering in alarm.

Cap whirled around, his right hand on the Colt. He glimpsed movement across the creek. At first he wondered if a squirrel had leaped from a low branch, but then he saw a buckskin-clad figure sprint through the trees as quickly and soundlessly as a fish through water. He advanced a step, halting when a familiar voice came from behind him.

"Don't shoot her, Cap."

Joshua Potter emerged from among the dark trees and lifted his army-issue Spencer repeater in a signal. White Moon Woman appeared across the creek to Cap's left, Bowie knife in hand.

Their strategy was effective, Cap realized. White Moon

Woman had distracted him, while Potter moved in. Had Cap been an enemy, he would be dead by now.

"Welcome to our neck of the woods," Potter said with a grin.

Cap grasped his outstretched hand. "I have already worn out my welcome, Joshua."

"Bluecoats on your trail?" he asked.

Cap stared at him. "How did you know?"

Potter jerked his head at White Moon Woman. "She's been frettin' all morning, grabbing my arm, and trying to tell me we have to leave. I figured she heard troopers, or smelled them, or something. Besides, I knowed Sully wouldn't quit on me. He's a prideful man."

White Moon Woman waded the creek. Sheathing the Bowie knife, she cast a tentative smile at Cap. He reached out and grasped her hand in greeting.

Turning to Potter, Cap quickly recounted the events since they had parted. He told him what had happened after Sully rode onto his homestead claim with a detachment of cavalry and Stanley Ashworth in tow.

"Are Jane and Jamie still sharing your camp?" Cap asked.

Potter nodded. "Left them in the lean-to with the baby after we heard the gunshot."

"I aim to get Ashworth off their backs," Cap said, "without putting any of you in harm's way. I need to talk to Jane right away."

Potter signed to White Moon Woman. She led them away from the creek, angling through the forest. On the way Cap described his whispered conversation with Marcus and the other troopers last night.

"Yeah, I know those ol' boys," Potter replied, chuckling as he walked behind White Moon Woman. "They know how to bust camp, yes, suh. But they's good soldiers, ever' one of 'em."

White Moon Woman continued to lead them on a serpentine path through the ancient forest. Like a whispering voice, the stream gurgled unseen through the dense underbrush. Then, in the morning shade, Cap saw a sheer rock face stretching skyward.

Even if he could have found it, the lean-to was so cleverly hidden in the brush and trees under the cliff overhang that he could have walked within fifty feet without seeing it. Potter gestured downstream and told Cap his horse was concealed below in a brush corral.

The sound of his deep voice brought Jamie lunging out of the lean-to. Jane followed out behind him, ducking to protect the baby in her arms.

"Cap! Cap!"

Cap turned, smiling as the boy ran toward him with a Winchester in his hands. "We heard a shot! Who's shooting?"

Cap grinned and shook his hand. The boy's face was ruddy, his grip strong. "I couldn't locate you, so I fired off a round."

Jane moved to his side. Her clothes were tattered, but clean, and she wore her hair braided now, Cheyenne fashion.

"Looks like you two are doing all right," Cap said.

"White Moon Woman is teaching us how to live in the wilderness," Jamie said excitedly. "She showed me how to catch trout and dry the meat. And I know where to find root vegetables."

Cap heard the infant murmur. White Moon Woman took the baby from Jane and handed him to Cap.

"Hello, my young friend," he said.

Cap gazed at the small, alert face he had first seen in this same blanket. The black-haired infant drooled and appeared to be attempting a toothless smile. Cap handed the baby back to White Moon Woman while Potter looked on.

"Getting heavy. He'll be bigger than his daddy one day."

"Yes, suh," Potter said, chuckling.

Cap turned to Jane. He told her Colonel Sully had been summoned by Ashworth, and troopers were now camped in the mountains not far from here.

"We'll fight that bastard!" Jamie exclaimed, lifting the repeater. "We won't go with him. . . ."

Jane shook her head and gave him a cautionary look.

"I see two choices," Cap said. "Hide from the man, or beat him at his own game."

Jane looked at him. "Beat him at his own game . . . how?"

"Go to Colonel Sully," he replied, "and testify against Ashworth. Sully represents the law in the territory. When he hears what you and Jamie have to say, he'll send Ashworth packing."

"But what if he doesn't?" Jane asked.

"We'll fight him . . . ," Jamie began.

"It's me the colonel's after," Potter broke in. "Ain't that right, Cap?"

Cap turned to him. "That's why I came to warn you. There's still enough time to put some distance between you and Sully."

Potter suggested: "Miss Reynolds, you and Jamie come with us. We'll dodge them troopers."

Jane shook her head. "Thank you, Joshua, but we would only place all three of you in danger. Cap's right. We'll be safe with the Army."

Jamie lowered his rifle. "But, Sis. . . ."

"This is a hard decision," she said, cutting Jamie off. "But I know Daddy would want us to face Stanley Ashworth."

"He'd want me to bring my gun, too!" Jamie said, hefting it in both hands.

Jane went to the lean-to to gather their belongings and load the rucksacks. When she emerged, she went to White Moon

Woman. The two women embraced.

"I don't know how to tell you in your language," Jane said, "but I hope you understand my gratitude. Jamie and I will never forget you."

White Moon Woman spoke in a soft voice. She smiled when Jane kissed the baby.

Leaving White Moon Woman in the camp, they followed Potter through the forest. When they reached the gelding, Cap tightened the cinch and helped Jane into the saddle. Jamie swung up behind her, his rifle across his legs.

"Good bye, Joshua," Jane said. "We'll never forget all you have done for us."

"You be careful now," he said.

Cap shook Potter's hand, and they parted. Walking with the reins in his hand, he led the horse to the creek and stepped into the water that quickly numbed his feet. He splashed through the shallow creek all the way to the beaver dams, leaving no trail. With the roar of the waterfall in his ears, he led the horse through the high grass into the lodgepoles on the slope of the ridge. Stopping there, he went back and covered their trail as best he could.

He led his horse upslope through the stand of arrow-straight lodgepole pines. In a clearing near the summit, the gelding suddenly tossed his head and shied. Jamie leaped free, the Winchester in his hands, while Jane kept a white-knuckled grip on the saddle horn.

Cap brought the big horse down. He looked upslope, but saw nothing. The buckskin tried to rear again. At Cap's urging, Jane hurriedly dismounted, landing on her feet.

"What is it, Cap?"

He shook his head. Holding the reins with one hand, he drew his Colt. He figured a bear or wolf lurked ahead, and the horse had caught scent of a predator. But then the sound of drumming hoofbeats reached him. The rumbling noise grew louder.

Moments later the troopers charged over the crest of the ridge. Jane shrieked in alarm. She turned and grabbed Jamie. They were quickly surrounded by half a dozen cavalrymen amid clouds of dust stirred up by the shod hoofs.

Cap saw the faces of the Ninth Cavalrymen, every trooper holding a Spencer carbine. A burly sergeant shouted, ordering Cap to holster his revolver.

Cap complied, and cast a glance back at Jane. Her eyes were wide with amazement and fear. So were Jamie's. In the next moment his attention was drawn to the crest of the mountain by the pounding hoofs of another horse.

Major Luke Symington topped the ridge and galloped out of the trees to the clearing. He rode through the line of troopers and hauled back on the reins.

"Hand over your weapons!" he ordered.

Cap did not obey. When the command was repeated, he said: "You have no authority to disarm us."

"Tell that to Colonel Sully," Symington replied.

Cap glimpsed Jamie raising his Winchester.

"Comes a time," Symington said, "when a soldier has to follow orders he dislikes."

Cap heard the steely tone of determination in the major's voice. He caught Jamie's eye and shook his head. Unbuckling his gun belt, he handed his holstered Colt to the nearest trooper.

Red-faced anger flared in Jamie's face. The boy was ready to do battle, Cap realized, just as his father would have been in this predicament.

He stepped closer to Jamie. "We'll go along with the major."

After a long hesitation Jamie nodded. Cap took the Winchester from him and tossed it to a trooper. Jane hugged her brother, tears of relief shining in her eyes.

Symington led the way. With Jane riding double behind him, Cap followed the major back to the encampment. Jamie rode double with a trooper. Cap turned and winked at his riding partner, trying to signal more confidence than he felt. Jane answered with a tight smile.

At dusk the riders were challenged by the sentries posted around the camp. In response to the warning shouts came a password from the sergeant. Then a pair of troopers on guard duty emerged from the cover of the trees, their carbines at the ready.

Symington spurred his horse and galloped ahead. Cap watched as he rode through a break in the trees that opened into the encampment. Reddish-orange glints from the campfires flickered and the pungent odors of woodsmoke and boiling coffee filled the air.

Escorted into the encampment, Cap saw that Colonel Sully had held the main body of troopers here, no doubt awaiting the outcome of Symington's pursuit. The men in Sully's command observed the riders filing past on their way to the base of the knoll.

Sully was there, conferring with Major Symington who still held his horse's reins. The colonel stood beside a blazing campfire, hands on his hips. He turned toward the approaching riders when Cap urged his horse ahead, ignoring the sergeant's shouted order to halt.

Cap saw another figure on the knoll, a small man edging to Sully's side. With his spectacles reflecting the firelight, Cap recognized Stanley Ashworth who folded his arms over his chest.

Cap reined up at the base of the knoll. "Get Ashworth out of here."

From his high ground position, Sully regarded him. "The day has not dawned that I'll take orders from you, McKenna."

"I didn't bring Jane Reynolds here to be bullied by that man," Cap said. "Get him out of here."

"You make it sound like you came in voluntarily," the colonel said, rocking back on his heels. "My major just told me otherwise."

"I was on my way to your encampment with Jane and Jamie," Cap said, "when Symington charged in."

"Another of your clever tales," the colonel said. "Fact is, you sneaked out of camp last night to warn Sergeant Potter. My troopers ran you down and brought you in . . . under guard."

"Colonel," Cap said, "you gave me no choice. You claimed you wanted to interview Jane and Jamie Reynolds. If you had pursued them with cavalry, you wouldn't have caught sight of them."

"As I say, McKenna, you spin a good yarn." Sully turned to the major. "Shackle him."

"Colonel!" Jane shouted. She jumped to the ground and started up the knoll, pointing at Ashworth. "He's the man you should arrest!"

"Miss Reynolds," Sully said, "calm down. I know you have an on-going dispute with Mister Ashworth. It will be resolved in due time."

"Dispute!" she said angrily. "He will stop at nothing to take over Reynolds Overland. He threatened us with our lives. . . ."

"You will be granted a hearing after supper, Miss Reynolds," Sully interrupted. He turned to Symington and repeated his order.

Cap did not resist when a trooper took the reins of his horse and led him away. He glanced back and saw Jamie join his sister on the side of the knoll. The evening light was thin, but not dark enough to conceal their distraught expressions.

Cap was taken to the middle of the encampment. When he dismounted, his hands were bound in front of him with steel shackles connected by a short length of chain. He sat down in the grass.

An hour later he was given coffee in a tin cup and a plate of bacon and beans. The trooper who brought the food was Marcus. Accompanied by a captain, Marcus pointedly avoided Cap's gaze.

Stars appeared in the night sky. Cap lay back in the grass and watched them. He figured the colonel was questioning Jane and Jamie now, asking more about the whereabouts of Potter than for details of their "dispute" with Ashworth.

He dozed, but was soon awakened by the nudge of a boot toe in his stomach. He opened his eyes to darkness. A shadow moved across him. As his eyes adjusted to the dark, the shadow took on definition and he saw that Ashworth stood over him.

Cap sat up. "Get out of here."

"Now you're the one who is in no position to give orders."

Cap struggled to his feet. "Shackles won't stop. . . ."

"Hear me out."

"I told Sully to keep you away from me."

"This is between us. Just hear me out. I want to make amends . . . and a deal."

"No deals."

"Mind your own affairs. That's all. Stay on your homestead. Offer testimony to no one. Your co-operation will earn you one thousand dollars . . . cash."

When Cap did not reply, Ashworth demanded: "Well?"

"I was just wondering," Cap replied, "how far one thousand dollars will fit up your ass."

"Don't be a fool," he said. "We have everything to lose . . . you and me."

"Sounds like a threat."

"Make trouble for me," he said, "and I'll finish the job started by that grass fire on your homestead claim. Fact is, if I don't get control of Reynolds Overland, the company won't be worth a cent, anyway. Not one damned cent."

"Go crawl back into your hole," Cap said.

Ashworth turned and strode away, fading into the night.

Chapter Thirteen

Cap slept fitfully, troubled by dreams at once vivid and confused. In the moments of first awakening, jumbled images slid away, leaving him with a sensation of detachment as though he had become a stranger in an unknown land. The cold bracelets quickly reminded him of his situation and brought him fully awake in the darkness before the dawn.

He heard the low voices of troopers in a last changing of the guard. He sat up, aware now that he had dreamed of war. Instead of his fallen comrades in Company B, the faces of Hezekiah and Jamie lingered in dream-like images. Wearing clean blue uniforms, the two youths charged to their deaths in the roar and stench of battle at Cedar Creek.

The loud snap of a dead branch broken over a trooper's knee took the dream memories away. Smoke billowed as men stoked the campfires. After breakfast Jane and Jamie joined him, sitting side by side in the dew-moistened grass, while the troopers broke camp around them.

Jane reached out and touched the shackles. "I did everything I could to convince the colonel that Ashworth is the one who should be confined in irons."

"Colonel Sully thinks Indians will attack," Jamie announced. "I need my gun."

Jane explained: "The colonel asked several times if Joshua had taken up with a tribe."

"And he wanted to know where Joshua's camp is," Jamie burst in, eyes narrowing. "But we didn't tell him."

Casting a motherly-like warning at Jamie, Jane continued:

"I'm afraid he'll follow our tracks to the beaver ponds, and search the forest."

"White Moon Woman will hear them coming," Jamie assured her.

Jane nodded as if she hoped it were true.

Jamie leaned in close to Cap. "If Joshua is captured, will he be hanged?"

Cap shook his head. "In peacetime a deserter is locked up in a stockade. After a hearing, he can be fined and reduced in rank . . . or dishonorably discharged."

"Or whipped like a slave!" Jamie said.

Jane agreed. "We saw the welts on his back."

Jamie stood. After looking around, he wandered to the brook. Cap saw Jane's eyes follow her brother's movements as he knelt down and tossed twigs into the slow current.

"We're alone in the world," she said softly. She turned to Cap. "That's why he's trying so hard to be a man."

On the crest of the knoll across the way Cap saw a number of junior officers conferring with Sully. Stanley Ashworth stood a short distance from them. Presently Colonel Sully left them and came down the slope. He strode through the encampment, his gaze on Cap.

"I wish to speak to Mister McKenna," Sully said when he reached them. "Alone."

Jane stood, her lips pursed into a thin line. "Colonel, isn't there anything I can say . . . ?"

"Return to my campfire. Both of you."

Jane gestured to her brother, and, with a glance at Cap, they walked away.

Sully was in full uniform from campaign hat to blackened boots. He gripped his gloves in one hand as he stood over Cap.

"This fine morning you have the opportunity to get rid of

those irons, Mister McKenna. Lead me to Potter, and you'll be a free man."

"I'm not your hound, Colonel," Cap said.

"You'd be well advised to reconsider your misplaced loyalties . . . to Potter as well as to Miss Reynolds."

"What're you driving at?"

"Mister Ashworth is a reputable attorney," Sully said. "After he appeared in my field camp in Denver and related his story, I sent a wire to Chicago. The man has a sterling reputation in northern Illinois. He tells me his sole wish is to protect the interests of the Reynolds heirs."

"The man's a liar," Cap said. "Since the death of her father, Jane Reynolds has been threatened and beaten by him."

"That's her story," Sully said.

"Confirmed by Jamie," Cap said.

"A twelve-year-old," he said with a shrug, "who echoes his sister's wild accusations."

"Jamie knows what he has seen and heard. . . ."

Sully waved the gloves impatiently. "Mister Ashworth wants to make peace with you. Says he owes you an apology, and regrets the actions of his hired guards. He hopes you can settle your differences."

"Take these irons off my wrists," Cap said, "and we'll settle our differences."

Sully dismissed his words with another wave of the gloves. "McKenna, with or without your help, my trackers will locate Potter's camp."

Sully started to walk away, but then he turned back. "Mister McKenna, it is my observation, you were once a man of honorable character. You achieved your moment in the sun during the war. Now you seem determined to play the rôle of a fool. Pity."

Cap watched the detachment ride out. Advance riders were under the command of Luke Symington. Cap scanned the troopers and saw Marcus, eyes front. He was uncertain if the man regretted aiding him, or if he was being cautious, merely taking care not to reveal anything to white officers.

After the last mounted trooper was gone, Jane and Jamie joined Cap. The morning passed with Jamie adding sticks occasionally to the campfire. A pair of troopers, assigned to watch them, sat in the grass thirty yards away. Others took up sentry positions in the trees around the meadow. The remaining men guarded the spare horses, pack animals, and the military gear and supplies. They rotated every two hours.

Lieutenant John Lowe commanded the detail. As the morning wore on, he moved between Cap and the knoll, clearly under orders to watch, but not fraternize, with the prisoner. He answered only one question posed by Cap: Stanley Ashworth was in the officer's camp on the back side of the knoll.

"See that he stays there," Cap said, but the young officer made no reply.

He remembered meeting Lowe at the officer's mess in the cavalry encampment outside Denver. After the meal the lieutenant had tamped tobacco into a pipe and smoked while sipping brandy. Cap had shaken his hand as the officers filed out of the mess tent and retired.

The day passed slowly. Jane and Jamie slept off and on, lying in the grass at the fire's edge. Cap looked at their faces in repose, seeing something of their father in both of them.

Coyotes yipped at dusk. Cap doubted Sully would return this day. The troopers would be forced to halt at nightfall. In the morning, Cap figured, Sully's trackers would search in vain for a trail. In all likelihood, the colonel and his mounted patrol would return late tomorrow, empty-handed.

At sundown he discovered he was wrong. A sentry's challenge pulled his gaze toward the fringe of pines to the west. He heard horses.

"What's happening?" Jane whispered, as she and her brother stared at the treeline.

A moment later troopers rode out of the forest like ghosts out of deep shadows. Major Symington's riders were followed into the encampment by the main party.

In the failing light Cap recognized Colonel Sully. The troopers filed past. Then he saw their prisoner — a large, broad-shouldered man, bare head bowed, hands lashed to the saddle horn.

Jane gasped softly. Jamie slowly stood, his mouth open in disbelief.

"Mister McKenna!" Sully called out in a booming voice. He turned his horse and rode toward the campfire. "We completed our mission without so much as a shot fired. The United States Army pursued and captured its prisoner."

Cap heard the gloating tone in his voice. He looked past the colonel at Joshua Potter.

"You will be happy to learn those irons are coming off you," Sully went on. "Sergeant Potter will be wearing them. At daybreak your horse and gear will be returned to you, and you will go back to your homestead." He repeated: "At daybreak."

"What about us?" Jane asked.

"You both shall remain in my custody for now," Sully said, and turned his horse. He rode to the knoll, calling for Lieutenant Lowe to release Cap and shackle Potter.

Jane and Jamie left the fire, hurrying to Joshua Potter. He was off the horse now and had raised his head to gaze at them. Jane reached out. She put her hand on his arm.

Lieutenant Lowe jogged across the meadow, unlocked the irons from Cap's wrists, and took them to the prisoner. Shackled, Potter was led away. Jane and Jamie, horrified by the goings-on, returned to Cap's fire.

"White Moon Woman and the baby are safe," Jane whispered, her cheeks wet with tears. "The troopers never found the lean-to. Joshua said it was when he was returning for his horse that he got caught."

After breakfast Symington came for them. "Colonel wants to see you . . . all of you."

Flanked by Jane and Jamie, Cap followed the major to the crest of the knoll. All of the command's officers, except Sully, were clustered around the blazing fire, tin cups of steaming coffee in their hands. Ashworth stood a dozen paces away, watching intently through eyes magnified by the lenses of his spectacles.

"Attention!" Symington said.

Colonel Sully topped the crest of the knoll. "At ease, gentlemen," he said after returning the major's salute.

Sully addressed his officers, first explaining the purpose of this meeting. Then he turned to Jane and Jamie.

"I have listened to all sides of your dispute. It is clear to me this matter must be resolved in the Illinois courts. Therefore, I order all parties to return to Chicago without delay."

"No!" Jamie shouted, jabbing his fist toward Ashworth. "No. . . ."

Jane put her arm around him. "We won't go anywhere with him, Colonel. You cannot force us. . . ."

"Calm down!" Sully said with sudden anger. "I am prepared to guarantee your safety."

Cap saw Jane purse her lips.

"I hereby order all parties to leave the territory," he went on. "The Ninth Cavalry will provide escort to Denver. Miss Reynolds, you and your brother will leave on the first coach to Cheyenne, Mister Ashworth on the next. From there, you will travel, separately, by train to Chicago."

Both Jane and Jamie started to protest, but Sully silenced them with a wave of his hand.

"Miss Reynolds, I shall send a message by wire. Federal officers in Illinois will meet your train. They will protect you and your brother from all danger." He added: "Real or imagined."

Ashworth chuckled.

Jane threw a sharp glance at the lawyer, and whirled to face Sully. "Colonel, do you think I made up everything I told you . . . that my brother and I have lied to you about this man?"

"Your veracity is not an issue for me to judge, Miss Reynolds. As I told you, your safety is assured."

She slowly shook her head. "You can't make us go."

"I can, Miss Reynolds, and I will. As commanding officer in this territory, I am obligated to uphold federal law. My decision is predicated on the fact that you must return to Illinois to resolve a legal issue. The manner in which you return is up to you . . . voluntarily, or under arrest."

Colonel Sully turned to Cap. "As for you, Mister McKenna, I now order you to quit this camp." He turned to his officers. "Dismissed, gentlemen."

With a last salute, the colonel moved off the crest of the knoll. He was striding downslope toward the officers' camp when Cap caught up with him.

"Colonel!"

Sully halted. He turned, his face dark with anger. "We have nothing further to discuss, Mister McKenna."

"Who will you answer to," Cap demanded, "when Ashworth takes his revenge on Jane and Jamie?"

Sully glared at him.

"When it's too late, you'll know he lied."

"Lied," Sully repeated in disgust. "Ashworth has been straightforward in our conversations. You're the one who has lied to me, McKenna . . . and more than once."

Cap raised his fist and advanced a step.

"McKenna!"

He stopped at the sound of Symington's voice behind him. Looking back, he saw the major standing a few paces upslope, revolver in hand. Other officers were bunched behind him.

Sully ordered: "Major, see that McKenna rides out of here. Without delay."

Cap lowered his fist as the colonel turned and strode downslope to the officers' camp. Symington holstered his side-arm. He closed the distance between them, gesturing to a rope corral holding the officers' mounts.

"Your horse and gear are over there," he said.

Cap found his gelding standing with the cavalry mounts. His saddle, saddlebags, canteen, blanket, and bridle were on the ground nearby. While Symington looked on, he caught his horse and pulled the bridle over his ears and then saddled him.

"Where's my rifle and gun belt?" Cap asked, leading the gelding out of the corral.

"Your weapons will be returned to you when we pass your cabin on our way to Denver," Symington said. He added: "Colonel's orders."

Cap stared at him. "Sully aims to send me out unarmed?"

"He claims you did the same to Mister Ashworth and his associates," Symington replied.

"The man's got him hook, line, and sinker, doesn't he?" Cap said. When Symington made no reply, he asked: "Which side do you come down on?"

"On the side of military discipline. I follow orders."

Cap tightened the saddle cinch, thrust a boot in the stirrup, and swung up. "I'll speak to Jane and Jamie on my way out of your field camp."

"No, you won't. The colonel ordered you to leave here directly."

"Then you'll have to shoot me out of the saddle."

"Hell, I'm not going to shoot you," Symington said. "I'm telling you for your own good . . . don't cross Tom Sully."

"You said that to me once before," Cap said, meeting his gaze. "In the Rocky Mountain Café."

"It was good advice then, too."

Cap shook his head. "I walked away from Joshua Potter that time. I don't aim to repeat the mistake."

He spurred his horse, riding to the crest of the knoll. Jane and Jamie stood by the fire. The officers had departed to break camp, taking Ashworth with them.

Cap drew rein. With a glance back, he saw Symington following, his jaw jutting out as he walked hurriedly to catch up.

"I have to leave. . . ."

"Take us with you!" Jamie said.

"I can't do you any good, if I'm a prisoner," he said. "You and Jane will have to stay with the troopers for now."

"What's going to happen to us?" Jane asked.

"I'll get a head start on this slow-moving cavalry," Cap said, "and find a way to help you. Tell Potter. . . ."

"McKenna!" Symington shouted as he topped the knoll behind him. "Ride out!"

Cap bid them good bye. He guided his horse down the slope to the meadow. He caught a single glimpse of Potter, mounted and under guard. He raised his hand in a wave, and

Potter answered with a nod of his head.

Cap left the meadow and rode thirty yards into the cool morning shadows cast by the spruce trees. Halting, he swung down. He quickly backtracked. Kneeling under a sagging bough, he watched as the troopers kicked out the campfires, checked weapons, and then stand to horse while awaiting the order to march.

A pine cone hit Cap in the back of his neck. Startled, he spun around, instinctively reaching for his Colt. His hand found an empty holster.

He saw White Moon Woman. She stood twenty paces away, smiling at him.

Chapter Fourteen

White Moon Woman carried a bow in her hand and a quiver of feathered arrows over her shoulder. The Bowie knife was sheathed on her belt.

Cap saw her gesture to her upper arm with three fingers and point toward the meadow. Her meaning was clear. She had come for Joshua Potter. In crude sign language Cap tried to explain that Potter was guarded, a prisoner of the bluecoats. Holding his wrists together, he pointed toward the encampment.

White Moon Woman looked at him curiously. She replied by drawing out the Bowie knife. She made a sawing motion, signaling her intention to cut Potter's bonds.

Cap shook his head again. He thought a moment, wondering how he could tell her that Potter's restraints could not be cut with a knife. In frustration he pointed to his brass belt buckle, then, gestured to his wrists. Next, by pointing at her knife, he tried to make it clear that the blade would not cut steel.

White Moon Woman nodded that she understood. But, pointing to her chest and then toward the encampment, she signaled her determination to free Potter. For emphasis she lifted the bow in a warrior's gesture.

Cap drew a deep breath. Clearly, she would risk her life for the man who had fathered her baby. And clearly, against the cavalry, she had no chance.

He wondered about the infant. Cradling his arms, he looked around in all directions, shrugging.

White Moon Woman understood. She smiled. Turning, she eagerly motioned: Follow me!

Cap led his horse through the trees as he walked behind her. Fifty yards away he discovered White Moon Woman had left her baby wrapped in the blanket under the cone-laden boughs of a pine. She knelt and lifted the bundle out. Turning to him, she opened the blanket. Cap moved closer. He looked down at the still face of the sleeping baby. The next moment he heard whinnying horses and loud voices.

Shouted orders drifted through the forest from the encampment. Cavalrymen were forming a column for the day's march. Cap looked at White Moon Woman. She had traveled with cavalry, and he could see she knew what was happening now, too. Distressed, she looked past him toward the sounds.

Cap caught her attention. He gestured to her: Come with me.

She shook her head and looked past him again.

Cap touched her arm. He motioned to his horse. With hand gestures he tried to signal her to ride double with him. She pulled away.

Come with me, Cap gestured again. He had not formulated a plan, but he knew he had to keep pace with the column.

At last she nodded. Relieved, Cap thrust a boot into the stirrup and mounted. When he reached down to pull her up, she thrust the baby to him. He took the bundle in his arms. White Moon Woman turned and ran.

Cap sat his saddle, shocked. He watched the lithe, buckskin-clad figure sprint through the trees toward the encampment, the quiver of arrows bouncing on her back. Then she was in the trees, out of his view. The baby whimpered.

Cap threw a leg over the saddle and slid to the ground. Holding the baby, he ran awkwardly toward a gap in the trees where he had last seen her. There, he caught sight of her ahead. She knelt between two pines, fitting an arrow into her bowstring. She pulled the sinew back. Before he could reach her, she let the arrow fly, and quickly drawing another from the quiver, she launched it, too. With amazing speed, she sent two more arrows whispering through the air.

Cap halted. Shouts erupted from the encampment as troopers spread word of an attack. Then came gunfire.

He hit the ground on one shoulder, protecting the baby as bullets whined past. Overhead branches were sliced, sending down showers of twigs and pine needles. He feared White Moon Woman would be shot, but, when he looked around, she was gone. As he rolled, trying to survey the area all around her while protecting the baby, he caught a glimpse of her, dashing to the left, almost concealed by the dense growth of trees. He stared as she knelt and launched more arrows, stood, and ran again. This time Cap lost sight of her. But he knew the arrows were finding marks. Horses squealed, and he heard the shrill voices of officers shouting orders.

Crouching, he scurried to his horse, grabbed the reins, and hurried into the trees, the baby clutched to his chest. Sporadic rifle fire continued for several minutes until the order — "Cease fire!" — was shouted.

The baby was suspiciously quiet. Cap lifted the blanket and looked inside to find the baby smiling at him. The infant's dark eyes were bright and unblinking, as though caught up in the excitement of the moment.

Distant shouts from cavalrymen came through the trees. Cap peered into the shadows, but the forest was too dark for him to see the column. But he heard hoofbeats. Moments later riders burst through the trees — Marcus and half a dozen cavalrymen. They were followed by Joshua Potter, hands still shackled as he grasped the saddle horn of his galloping horse.

Clearly they were not on the attack. Cap called to them.

They hauled back on the reins. Cap ran to Potter, whose face was distorted in amazement to find him here with the baby.

"Where is she?" Potter shouted. "Where's White Moon Woman? Did they shoot her?"

"I don't know," Cap replied.

In a voice excited by danger, Marcus said: "Ol' Josh, he told us that Indian woman would come for him. Damned if she didn't! Colonel took an arrow in his chest. Lieutenant Lowe hit, too." He drew a breath. "We figured a whole tribe was attacking, until Josh explained. So me and the boys, we just spurred our horses into the trees. . . ."

Beyond Marcus, Cap saw movement in the tangled forest shadows. "Look."

Potter's head snapped around. White Moon Woman appeared, running out of the forest toward them. She carried her bow. The quiver was empty now.

Breathing hard when she came up to them, White Moon Woman stopped at Potter's mount. He awkwardly reached down with both hands and pulled her up behind him.

Marcus swung his horse around and grasped Potter's arm. Digging in his spurs, he led the other troopers back into the trees, without a word, heading for the encampment at a gallop.

Cap handed the baby up to White Moon Woman, and caught his horse. Swinging up, he urgently gestured for Potter to follow.

Potter shook his head. "You go on, Cap. Me and White Moon Woman, we can lose the whole cavalry in these mountains."

Cap pointed to his wrists. "And wear those things for the rest of your life? We'll ride to the barn. I'll cut them off your wrists."

"Cap, we ain't got time. The colonel, he'll ride you down. I cain't put you up against him. . . ."

"My guess is Sully will order defensive positions," Cap replied, "until he figures out no more attacks are coming. That'll give us a head start, if we ride hard."

Cap hefted the five-pound sledge hammer in his right hand, while gripping a cold chisel in his left. Potter's arms were extended, his muscles flexing as he held the right wrist shackle down on the flat surface of the anvil.

Cap lifted the hammer. He brought it down, hard. With the first ringing blow the sharp chisel bit into steel. Cap kept pounding, striking the chisel until the blade cut through.

Potter lifted his hand and grinned. He removed that bracelet from his wrist, and then put down the other cuff on the anvil.

After Cap cut through it, Potter straightened up, rubbing both wrists. "Feels good to be a free man, mighty good."

Cap put the hammer down. "Hezekiah's cooking supper."

On their way out of the barn Potter asked about the youth who had stepped out of the cabin, pistol in hand, when they had arrived after dark. Cap related how they had met, and the circumstances that had brought him here.

Potter chuckled.

Cap sent a puzzled look at him.

"All manner of two and four-legged critters," Potter said, "have a knack for findin' you, Cap. Yes, suh."

Summer sausage and flapjacks were in the frying pan when they stepped into the cabin. Potter pulled out the small bench at the pine table. After Hezekiah served the food, he watched the big man eat hurriedly.

"Danged shame I ain't got time to enjoy this meal," he said with a broad smile. "Young 'un, you cook up a fine mess."

Hezekiah motioned to the skillet. "There's enough for that Indian."

146

Cap had not seen White Moon Woman since she had taken the baby to the aspen grove upon their arrival at the cabin. Now Potter pushed back from the table and got to his feet.

"Slide that chow onto my plate, young 'un. I'll take it to her."

"Why does she stay outdoors?" Hezekiah asked. "I ain't against savages eating alongside us white folks." Embarrassed, he added: "Or black folks, neither."

Potter laughed, relieving Hezekiah's youthful embarrassment. He merely commented: "Reckon she's jumpy."

"Why?" Hezekiah asked.

"Troopers headed this way," he answered over his shoulder. Stopping in the doorway, he added: "Cap, soon as White Moon Woman eats, we'll ride."

Half an hour later Cap found them in the aspen grove. He stood by as Potter readied the horse and mounted, then he helped White Moon Woman up behind him.

"So long, Cap," Potter said, and shook his hand. "Thanks."

Cap looked at White Moon Woman holding her baby in the blanket. She smiled.

That smile, an expression of warmth and trust crossed the barrier of language, communicating more than words could convey. Cap wondered if she knew she had thrown a mighty scare into him when she had thrust the baby in his arms and ran to attack the cavalry with nothing but a bow and quiver of arrows. She might have died in those moments of attack, and he felt honored that she had entrusted her baby to him.

Acts of bravery bordered on the insane, Cap knew, and were later celebrated by survivors. Anyone who had experienced that giddy surge after a close call had glimpsed a mystery: the thin line between life and death marked an emotional

147

landscape both strange and compelling, never understood, never forgotten.

He reached up and touched the baby one last time, and then they departed. Potter guided the horse into Trapper Creek, the horse's hoofs splashing as he rode away from the homestead without leaving a trail.

Cap had listened to his plan. Potter would ride downrange several miles before turning west into the mountains. From there he would make his way back to the lean-to.

In the morning Cap and Hezekiah lugged buckets from Trapper Creek. They poured water into the horse trough next to the corral. Both the barn and corral had been built, at Cap's direction, some fifty yards upslope from the creekbed. Trapper Creek was small, but capable of flooding in the spring or even in a summer downpour, and this location protected both the barn and the animals inside.

Still fatigued from yesterday's ride, Cap set the wooden buckets down on the ground. He leaned back against the top pole of the corral and pushed his hat up on his forehead, feeling a bit of tenderness from the blow to the back of his head. He wiped his brow, while Hezekiah finished the job. Their path was marked by damp earth and shiny green grass where water had sloshed out of the buckets.

Hezekiah stopped abruptly. His gaze lifting, the buckets slipped from his grasp and toppled end over end. Water pooled around his boots.

Cap turned, following the youth's stare toward the slope behind the cabin. Mounted troopers emerged from the trees on top of the ridge. He straightened his hat with a painful tug on the brim, watching the blue-coated cavalrymen of the Ninth descend the ridge. When the riders drew closer, he recognized the lanky figure in the lead — Major Luke Symington.

"Advance scouts," Cap said, "in Sully's column."

Hezekiah picked up the empty buckets and hurried toward the corral and Cap. "What's gonna happen?"

"Don't know," Cap replied. "I can't put up much of a fight, until they give my guns back to me."

Hezekiah cast an alarmed look at him, and then grinned sheepishly when he saw the slight smile on Cap's beard-stubbled face.

Symington galloped ahead of the others. He rode into the yard and halted at the corral. He did not answer Cap's greeting.

"We ran into a little trouble yesterday," Symington said from the saddle. "Savages hit us."

"How many?" Cap asked.

The major shrugged, eyeing him. "Some of the men say it was only one. Hit-and-run. Struck fast and disappeared before we could mount a counterattack. Tom Sully's wounded. So's Lowe." He paused. "In the confusion of battle, Potter escaped."

Cap met the major's gaze in silence.

"The colonel believes you used your military expertise to orchestrate the attack."

"Major, I had nothing to do with it."

Symington exhaled tiredly. He looked back the way he had come. "You can tell Tom yourself . . . if he's in a frame of mind to listen."

Cap shifted his attention to the ridge again. Riders emerged from the treeline along the top, a double line of troopers flanked by scouts, all of them moving slowly downslope.

Cap asked Symington: "The colonel hurt bad?"

"Arrow caught him high in the chest," he replied. "Not deep. But Tom's in pain."

Cap studied Symington. Frustration and fatigue etched the

149

man's face. Cap figured Symington disagreed with Sully's purpose for the expedition, but was not one to openly criticize his commanding officer.

"The day we left the Platte encampment our surgeon was too drunk to ride," Symington went on. "So yesterday I had to yank that arrow out of Tom's chest myself, leaving the flint point in him. Poured whiskey on the wound and bandaged it as best I could, while he drained the flask."

The troopers drew closer. Hezekiah watched with great interest as the cavalrymen bivouacked near the bank of Trapper Creek. Major Symington reined his horse around and rode past the cabin to meet them near the aspen grove.

Ashworth rode with a corporal at the front of the formation. Next came the commanding officer, bent forward in the saddle, dark red stains marking the front of his uniform. Lieutenant Lowe appeared to be in better shape. Cap watched him ride to the creek and dismount, unassisted. Sully needed help when his horse halted at water's edge.

"Cap!"

Jane and Jamie brought up the rear of the formation, riding spare cavalry mounts. They broke off and rode to the corral.

Jamie waved his hat over his head. "Cap! Cap!"

Cap grinned, noting the same full-steam-ahead rush for life he had seen in J. Stuart Reynolds. His eyes went to Jane. Riding at a high lope toward him, she stayed close to her brother.

"Indians attacked us!" Jamie said when he reached the trough.

"It happened so fast . . . ," Jane began.

"We didn't even have time to get scared!" Jamie finished the sentence for her.

Still grinning, Cap helped Jane down.

She eyed him. "You don't seem much concerned."

150

He looked at her for a moment, recalling the first time he had set eyes on her. She had stepped out of the surrey and tilted her head up to face him. Her complexion had been creamy white. She had changed a great deal in a short time, now toughened and tanned, yet still pretty.

He introduced Jane and Jamie to Hezekiah. When Hezekiah took their reins to tend the horses, Jamie eagerly volunteered to help him.

"What about Joshua?" Jane said after the two boys left for the barn. "Is he . . . is he . . . ?"

"He's alive."

She studied him again. "Cap, you know more than you're telling, don't you?"

"I know the Ninth Cavalry was attacked by a woman warrior," he said very quietly.

She stared in amazement, while he recounted the fast-moving events that unfolded after he had left the encampment, careful to keep his back to the soldiers along the creek.

"I . . . I don't know whether to laugh or cry," she said, her hands moving to her cheeks. "Do you mean White Moon Woman . . . ?" Her voice trailed off as this information sunk in.

"I mean she fired her arrows at white officers," Cap said, "and, with help from a handful of troopers, she did exactly what she said she was going to do . . . set Potter free."

Cap suggested they go to the cabin, and, once inside, he stirred the coals in the stove and rekindled the fire. Jane stretched out on the bunk, eyes closed until Hezekiah loudly charged in with Jamie close behind him.

"Cap, that 'ere stranger's snoopin' in the barn."

"What stranger?"

"He wears spectacles."

"That damned bastard, Ashworth," Jamie said, following

151

Hezekiah through the doorway.

Jane sat upright. "Jamie, that's no way to talk. . . ." Her reprimand was cut off, when Cap rushed past her and ran out the door.

He jogged to the open doors of the barn, wishing for his revolver. He stepped inside and halted. "Ashworth!" he called out. Met with silence, he eased into the runway, catching only the soft sounds of horses in their stalls. His eyes adjusted to the dim light in the cool and cavernous barn, and then he went about peering into the tack room and the individual stalls. Next, he climbed the ladder to the mow and searched it. Stanley Ashworth was not among the bales of hay or sacks of grain stored there.

Unsettled, Cap returned to the cabin. He was met by Jamie at the door.

"Don't let Colonel Sully take us to Denver," he said. "Please, Cap. We want to stay here."

Before Cap could reply, Symington hailed him as he strode out of the aspen grove with Cap's rifle and revolver. He walked to the cabin in silence and handed the weapons to him.

"Colonel Sully wants to see you."

Placing a reassuring hand on Jamie's shoulder, Cap turned and made his way to the grove. Symington led him through the trees to the brush shelter constructed by White Moon Woman. Colonel Sully, jacket off now, reclined in the shade of the structure. The command's officers gathered nearby. Ashworth stood behind them.

Sully sat up, groaning against the pain from his wound. His face was drawn. On the right side of his chest his undershirt bore bloodstains where it bulged over a thick bandage.

"I'm placing you under arrest, McKenna."

"Arrest," Cap repeated. "On what charge?"

"Conspiring with savages to attack troopers in my command."

"I had nothing to do with. . . ."

"In addition," Sully interrupted, "you are charged with aiding the prisoner in his escape. Don't bother to concoct a tale to deny it."

Cap heard the note of triumph in the colonel's strained voice, the same tone he had heard after the capture of Joshua Potter.

Sully groaned again as he shifted his upper body and lifted his hand in a beckoning gesture. Cap watched as Stanley Ashworth moved closer to the brush shelter. Metal clinked as he held up two steel objects.

"You chiseled those irons off Potter," Sully said, "and set him loose. That's the truth, isn't it, McKenna?"

Cap understood now, too late, what Ashworth had been doing in the barn. The man was shrewd. He must have remembered seeing the anvil, sledge hammer, and horseshoeing tools on his previous visit with Archie and Leonard, when they slept in the tack room. Cap's homestead was the only place from here to the blacksmith shop in Denver where wrist irons could be cut.

"We leave at dawn, McKenna," Sully said. "This time you won't escape prosecution in federal court."

Chapter Fifteen

The cavalry encampment on the bank of the South Platte River hummed with mosquitoes. Cap was confined to a tent within stink distance of a latrine trench on the far edge of camp. He was not bound, but he was guarded around the clock.

He had been told Jane and Jamie were staying in a room in the Denver House, prepared to leave town in the first available stagecoach. Ashworth would remain behind and board the next Cheyenne-bound coach, an important part of the promise Sully had made in an effort to guarantee the safety of the sister and brother.

In between scratching himself, Cap plucked green willow branches and built a smoky fire to ward off the mosquitoes. Often in his idle hours he found himself thinking of the waitress in the Rocky Mountain Café. Something about the way she had looked at him with a smile in her eyes had stayed with him.

After supper was brought by Marcus, Cap sipped coffee from a dented, smoke-stained cup. He asked who was guarding Jane and Jamie.

"None of *us* boys," the trooper answered.

The answer surprised Cap. "Sully said they would be guarded by the Ninth."

"Don't know about that, suh. Black folks ain't allowed near the Denver House. Nowheres near, no, suh."

"Where's Ashworth?"

"He ain't in camp," Marcus said with a shrug. He studied

Cap for a moment, then asked: "You planning to bust camp?"

Before Cap could answer, a guard nearby whistled. Marcus quickly stood and moved away.

Cap saw Symington approaching. The major strode between two rows of tents to Cap's campfire. He knelt and delivered a message. Colonel Sully, even though exhausted and in pain, had issued one last order before the surgeon had administered a healthy dose of morphine: "The prisoner will receive no visitors."

"He sent you all the way over here just to tell me that?" Cap asked.

Symington looked him straight in the eye. "Tom is convinced you and some troopers aided Potter in his escape. He wants me to question you."

"Can't trust his own men, is that it?"

Symington hesitated. "Commanding Negroes on the frontier is a difficult task. Difficult at best. They are free men, yet they are not free as white men are." He added: "At times they seem to hate us."

Cap saw him cast a pensive look at the rows of evenly spaced tents.

"If you know anything," Symington continued, as he turned to face Cap, "tell me. Co-operate, and I'll urge Tom to drop charges and let you go back to your homestead. I feel certain he can be persuaded. . . ."

"I have nothing to say."

"Don't underestimate Tom Sully. . . ."

"What I want to know," Cap broke in, "is who's protecting Jane and Jamie?"

"You needn't worry. They're well taken care of."

"Your troopers aren't allowed in the Denver House," Cap said.

"True," Symington conceded. "Our officers enjoy the privilege of sleeping in a real bed and taking meals in the restaurant. They'll look out for Miss Reynolds and young Jamie."

"So will Ashworth," Cap said. "Where is he?"

"That's not your affair," Symington said. He stood and walked away.

That night an infant's cries came to Cap in a dream. He awakened to darkness and silence in the small tent. In his state of half wakefulness he wished for a son, then drifted back to sleep until roused in the morning by the bugle.

After reveille, breakfast was brought by Marcus. From him, Cap learned that, when the morphine wore off last night, Colonel Sully woke up howling in pain. Cap recalled his dream. The distant cry of a man, not his dream of an infant, had awakened him.

At mid-morning as he lay in the small tent, slapping mosquitoes, when a shadow passed over the white canvas. The shadow stopped.

Cap opened the flap. "Symington."

Clearly troubled, the major did not speak for a long moment. Then he pulled off his hat and ran a hand through his short-cropped hair, a mannerism Cap had noted before when the man felt torn between his duty as an officer and a course of action he knew to be right.

"Miss Reynolds and young Jamie . . . ," he began. His voice trailed off. He cleared his throat. "Well, they're gone."

"Gone? They took the stage to Cheyenne?"

Symington shook his head. "They left the Denver House early this morning, before dawn. They rented a buggy. . . ."

Cap interrupted: "Where's Ashworth?"

"My officers reported to me that Ashworth had not come down for breakfast. They found his room empty. After inquiring around town, they interviewed a livery man who had rented saddle mounts to six men this morning . . . one was

156

short in stature, wearing silver-rimmed spectacles. He paid the bill, cash in advance."

"Who were the others?" Cap asked.

"River riff-raff," Symington replied, "along with Ashworth's two associates. Some of the men were reeling drunk. The livery man heard them boast of killing Indians." He paused and then added: "They all carried new Winchesters."

Cap scrambled out of the tent. "I have to talk to Sully."

"Tom's asleep."

"Wake him."

Symington replaced his hat and shook his head. "I wouldn't, even if I could."

"What the hell do you mean by that?"

"Tom's got enough morphine in him to drop a bull," Symington said.

"Ashworth's going after Jane and Jamie," Cap said. "He has threatened them. I figure he aims to kill them both . . . and claim they were murdered by Indians. Then he'll take over Reynolds Overland."

Symington eyed him doubtfully.

Cap went on: "Maybe we can agree on this much, Major. Every minute we stand here jawing gives Ashworth more time to overtake them."

"If you're suggesting I send out a detachment to track them down and bring them in," Symington said, "the answer is no. I have no authority to issue marching orders."

"I'm suggesting," Cap answered, "you return my gear so I can track them down. If Ashworth comes in peaceably, then we'll all know who's lying."

"McKenna, I can't release you from custody."

"You have my word," Cap said, "that no matter what happens, I'll ride back here to face the trumped-up charges."

Symington shook his head.

Exasperated, Cap said: "Even if I broke my word, you'd know where to find me. I'm not going to walk away from a homestead I've put my sweat and blood into for three years."

"I'm telling you, McKenna, it's not my decision," he said. "I have never violated a direct order from my commanding officer, and I won't start now. You will be confined here until Tom says otherwise. . . ."

Cap's fists had involuntarily clenched, and now, without thinking, he advanced a step.

Symington's eyes flickered in surprise. He squared his shoulders. "You will be well advised to back away."

"Man to man," Cap said.

"Don't do this."

"Either you're man enough to stop me from riding out," Cap said, "or you're not."

Cap saw him cast sidelong glances left and right. Word of their confrontation was passing from the guard through the camp like a wind-driven fire, and troopers were leaving their tents and coming toward them, slowly, with expectant looks on their faces.

"You've challenged me in front of men under my command, McKenna. Now you'll have to back down."

Cap watched the officer's flinty eyes. "No, Major. Now you'll have to stop me from riding out of here."

"This is not a fight I want, McKenna."

"Just as you wanted no part of Sully's vendetta?" Cap asked. "I figure that's what you had in mind when you said a time comes when a soldier has to obey orders he dislikes."

"My personal view has no bearing on this," Symington replied. "You're not leaving this camp. Those are my orders."

Cap started to walk past him, but Symington reached out and grabbed his shoulder. Cap knocked his hand away and whirled to faced him.

158

Eyes fixed on Cap, the major unbuttoned his tunic, pushing each brass button out of its buttonhole. He shouldered out of the garment and tossed it aside. Then he set his feet and raised his fists, arching his back in the posture of a pugilist.

Cap rocked forward slightly, his boots scraping dirt as he circled.

Symington quickly stepped in. He let go with a left jab, his right fist still cocked back to his chest.

Cap ducked the punch. It missed, but not by much. In a flash the right hand followed, and this time Cap felt knuckles graze his cheek. He backed away. Symington came after him. The two were nearly equals in weight and height. But now Cap knew this man was fast — fast and well schooled in the manly arts.

Cap's experience was limited to barroom brawls and tent camp battles from his days as an enlisted man in the Army. He had not fought often, but, when forced to, he fought by instinct.

His only plan was to hit hard and hope the major would give up the fight. Watching Symington's quick jab now, though, made him realize the man's approach was calculated and skilled, a physical chess match requiring strategy and patience.

Cap ducked one jab, and bobbed directly into a stiff right. Before he knew it, he was on the ground, head throbbing, dust in his mouth. He quickly got up, only to be hit by three more stinging jabs and another right that put him down. His face felt wet. When he wiped a hand across his mouth, it came away bloody. Cap staggered to his feet, his vision doubled. Blinking, he felt more confusion than weakness.

"Give it up, McKenna."

Cap tried to focus on Symington. When his vision cleared,

he saw the major standing four paces away, fists up, back arched. Cap shook his head.

"All right then," Symington said. He moved in, quickly closing the distance between them.

Cap recognized his previous mistakes. He had been hit every time he reacted to the jab. Ducking away from the left fist gave Symington his opening, and he used it to hit Cap with the right, his stronger punch.

This time Cap stood still, watching. When Symington stepped in and flicked his left fist, he did not move. The major paused. Jabbing again, he clearly expected Cap to duck. The light punches hit their mark. Symington was ready, right fist cocked, but Cap took more jabs without flinching. Symington stopped. He shifted his feet and feinted with the right.

At that moment Cap lunged, rifling his right fist into the major's face. The punch smashed him squarely in the mouth. Symington was rocked back, at once bleeding and dazed. A spontaneous cheer erupted from the troopers. Cap moved fast, coming in low with a punch to the abdomen. The blow landed with full force, doubling Symington over. Cap reached down and swung upward. The uppercut caught Symington flush in the face, standing him up. Eyes glazed now, his fists sank.

Cap set his feet and cocked his right arm. When Symington made a weak effort to jab, Cap hit him in the jaw, hard. The major spun around, arms flailing like ribbons in a breeze. Legs buckling, he went down. Cap bent forward, hands braced on his knees as he gasped for air. The taste of blood filled his mouth.

Flat on his back, Symington breathed shallowly as though asleep, his jaw purpling around a knot swelling to the size of a walnut.

Cap caught his breath. Straightening, he wiped his mouth with his bandanna. Troopers edged closer, smiling and speaking softly to one another, until they confirmed the major was out cold.

Marcus smiled broadly. "Yes, suh, the major, now ain't he a fancy fighter? Yes, suh. But you, Mistah Cap, damned if you don't pack a punch to knock a brick outen a wall."

"Yes, suh," echoed other troopers. "Yes, suh!"

Cap drew a deep breath and spat. "Help me get my horse and gear."

He did not take time to track Jane and Jamie on the rutted freight road. Riding out from the military camp on the Platte, he guessed they had ridden north. They had either headed to Cheyenne to board the next Chicago-bound train, or they had veered off the wagon road and followed Trapper Creek to the mountains.

Trapper Creek was his best guess. Cap believed Jane's strategy was to avoid Ashworth. By doing so, she and Jamie would feel safe and at once retain majority ownership of Reynolds Overland. If his theory was right, Jane and Jamie would hike into the mountains, figuring they could evade Ashworth until winter, if necessary. A city man could not hold out for long in the wilderness.

If Stanley Ashworth followed the same line of reasoning, Cap thought, he must know he faced a hard ride. He would have to move fast to close the distance, catching Jane and Jamie before they disappeared in "god-forsaken terrain."

The gelding was rested and up to the task. Cap thought he was, too, but after two hours in the saddle the effects of the fist fight were beginning to take their toll. He had won, but had taken a beating while doing it. His lips were puffed and his head was aching from the many bruises which were tender to the touch. A cut inside his mouth bled, and he had swallowed enough blood to feel nauseous. He spat and drank

161

the last of the water in his canteen.

Cap guided the horse off the wagon road. He rode through a stand of cottonwoods and drew rein at the bank of the Platte. He swung down. Kneeling in the mud, he filled his canteen from the slow-moving river, drank again, and splashed water over his head. It helped some. He wanted to strip and wade in, but he had no time for such luxury. He ate jerky and discovered a tooth loosened by Symington's fist. Therefore, Cap chewed gingerly and drank more water. The jerky softened. Still chewing, he mounted and rode back to the freight road. When he turned northward, the buckskin broke into a canter as though eager to be home. Cap's head pounded with the brisk gait.

He topped the low hill overlooking the Haynes farm. Drawing closer to the squat sod house, he saw Emily outside. She tipped a bucket, watering her red and white hollyhocks by the front door. Sounds of an approaching horseman made her straighten and turn, tilting her head until the brim of her sunbonnet shaded her eyes. The dog barked and slunk away.

"Afternoon, Missus Haynes," he said, pulling back on the reins.

"Oh, it's you," she said tentatively. She set the bucket down. "My Hezekiah still at your place?"

"Yes, ma'am," Cap said.

She paused. "After he met you, all he could talk about was that 'ere cowboy on that 'ere big cow horse. Said he'd have his own place one day and ride a big horse, too. Guess we all have to make the break . . . but I shore do miss my firstborn."

"He'll come back," Cap said.

She shook her head. "Not until Zeke gets his answer from God." Emily Haynes took a step closer. "Looks like you had the same sort of trouble Zeke had."

162

Cap raised a hand to his face, gingerly touching the bruises with his fingertips. "Disagreement with an Army officer."

"Army," she repeated. "Say, whatever happened to that 'ere tar baby you found in the bulrushes?"

"I returned him to his mother. He's fat and sassy, now."

She smiled briefly.

"Missus Haynes," Cap asked, "have you seen any north-bound travelers today?"

"Reckon so."

"A young woman and a boy . . . in a buggy."

"Seen 'em early this morning."

"What about riders?" Cap asked. "A bunch of toughs led by a man wearing spectacles?"

She nodded. "Seen them, too. Three, four hours ago."

With the western peaks cutting their jagged line in a star-filled sky, Cap reached Trapper Creek. He followed it to the foothills. The red glow on the horizon might have signaled sunrise, Cap thought, if the world had turned upside down. But this was nighttime and the rich red-orange color blossomed to the west, straight ahead, at the base of the foothills. Then came the smell of smoke, and the buckskin pranced.

Cap tightened the reins, stood in the stirrups, and peered ahead. Clouds of billowing smoke obscured the stars. He swore aloud.

The fire was a big one, and he knew beyond any doubt where it was. The flames leaped high into the sky from the shake roof of his barn. When he drew closer, he saw that his cabin was on fire, too, the logs burning brightly around the edges of the dirt roof.

Cap left his horse and leaped across Trapper Creek, now in hearing range of the soft but menacing roar. He raised a hand against the waves of heat. As he moved toward the conflagration, the firelight revealed a body sprawled on the ground. Cap ran. He skidded to his knees beside the prone figure. The patchy-bearded face was turned sideways, bloodied, eyes closed.

"Hezekiah," Cap whispered, coughing against the smoke. "Hezekiah!"

Chapter Sixteen

Cap lifted Hezekiah by the shoulders and dragged him downslope to the bank of Trapper Creek. The youth groaned. The towering flames cast shadows and light on his matted hair, revealing a bloody crease along the side of his head — a bullet wound. He stretched the boy out on the bank of the creek and washed the wound, catching a glimpse of white bone where the skin had been sliced open by the bullet in a long, neat line. After pulling it together and bandaging the wound with his bandanna, he sloshed handfuls of water over Hezekiah's face.

The youth slowly revived, making unintelligible sounds. Then he abruptly sat up, his gaze darting from Cap to the leaping flames and back again. As though awakening from a nightmare, he lashed out.

Cap grabbed his arms and restrained him. "It's all right. It's all right."

"He . . . he . . . shot me."

"Who?"

"Stranger . . . spectacles. . . ."

"Ashworth."

"Cap, he . . . he done burned us out."

Hezekiah told Cap what had happened, and now he knew enough to piece the events together. Jane and Jamie had been here. They stayed long enough to eat and rest. Then, leaving the buggy hidden in the aspen grove, they hiked up the ridge behind the cabin. Late in the night Hezekiah heard horses.

"That 'ere stranger . . . came out of the night . . . like

Satan hisself . . . riders . . . horses loose."

Rambling on about running horses and evil forces, Hezekiah passed out. Cap figured Ashworth's men had approached the homestead with caution. They drove the horses out of the barn to lure Hezekiah outside — along with anyone else who might have been in the cabin. The ruse worked. Awakened by hoofbeats, Hezekiah had run out, nearly colliding with the stranger who aimed a pistol at him and demanded to know if Jane and Jamie had been here. When Hezekiah nodded, Ashworth pulled the trigger.

Cap looked at Hezekiah's face by the light of flames, a youthful countenance, eyes closed, mouth slack. Memories of the war swept over him. As eager as he was to take up the chase, he could not leave Hezekiah here like a wounded soldier on the battlefield, perhaps to die.

By the time Cap had found the buggy and had shoved it out of the trees, his cabin had burned to the ground. The pines he had dropped, notched, and then stacked, shoulder high — as high as he was able to lift them by himself — were now charred, the fire reduced to low flames and glowing red coals. The roof had caved in, leaving the stove pipe up, but tilting to one side.

He found the team down Trapper Creek. The Reynolds plugs had scattered, but the pair of livery horses stood nose to hip on the far bank, a sensible distance from the flames. He easily caught them and hitched them to the buggy. Then he dragged Hezekiah to the vehicle, hoisting his upper body and shoving him onto the seat. The youth slumped over. Cap climbed in and shifted Hezekiah so that he lay half on his lap, half on the seat.

Driving away from the homestead, the sharp crack of breaking timbers drew his gaze back to the barn. He watched the shake roof and hay mow collapse, and heard a strangely familiar sound — a low, sad moan. Sparks and flares rocketed skyward, some disappearing in blackness while others spiraled to earth like orange-tailed comets. The mournful sound evoked an old memory. In his boyhood he had seen a sailing ship aflame in the Susquehanna River. The three-masted vessel had tipped back on its stern and moaned as it slipped into dark water — a dying sound once heard, never forgotten.

Cap reached the Haynes farm after moonrise. The team was not fast, but, with two horses pulling the light vehicle, he had made good time on the wagon road. Hezekiah rocked with the motion of the buggy, at times uttering sounds as though struggling to regain consciousness.

By moonlight the low soddy was a squat rectangle. As he approached, Cap heard barked warnings from the dog. He rolled into the yard and drew back on the lines, seeing Zeke Haynes in the doorway, shotgun in hand. Over the yapping dog, Cap loudly announced himself. He told Haynes Hezekiah was hurt.

Haynes came out of the doorway and paused. He was passed by Emily and the three boys, all of them in night-clothes, as they hurried to the buggy.

"What happened?" she demanded as she reached out for her son. "What happened?"

"He's been shot," Cap replied, and climbed down.

Between the three adults and with help from the boys, they carried Hezekiah into the sod house and laid him on the bed closest to the door. Haynes observed them wordlessly as the lamps were fired. The light glowed on the mother on her knees examining her son. She stroked his head and pressed his limp hand to her cheek.

Cap explained what he had discovered upon his return to his homestead, and had started to tell them about the riders led by Ashworth, when he felt a hard jab in his back. He turned. Haynes was pointing the shotgun at him.

"Git out of my house. Git out."

Haynes stood over a lamp on a low table with a black Bible. The flame cast shadows upward, from his bearded jaw to his rumpled hair standing on end, an image as fearsome as a mad prophet.

Cap walked to the door with Haynes, advancing step for step, the shotgun trained on his back. Outside the two men moved onto the footpath between the rows of hollyhocks.

"I'm going after the man who shot Hezekiah," Cap said. "I'll bring him to justice. . . ."

"Justice!" Haynes interrupted with a shout. "What can a heathen know of justice?"

Cap saw him clench the shotgun so tightly that it shook as though alive.

"As thunder is to the skies, so shall the wrath of God Almighty in His heaven deliver justice, yea, holy justice, swift and true."

Cap's mouth went dry as he searched for the words that might distract this man so clearly intent on committing murder.

"You flung the devil's own trickery upon my family," he went on. "Satan pits sons against fathers in unholy war. Now . . . *now!* . . . the flaming sword from heaven on high shall strike you down!"

Cap saw the big man draw a ragged breath as he jabbed the shotgun at him.

"Pray to God, heathen! Pray to God Almighty! Drop to your knees and pray to God Almighty. . . ."

"Zeke," Emily said from the doorway. She raised her voice. "Ezekial!"

She rushed to his side and grabbed his arm. He tried to shove her away, but she held on.

"Praise God!" she said. "Hezekiah spoke!"

Haynes kept his eyes on Cap.

"It's our message from God! Praise God Almighty!"

Her weathered face in profile showed both anguish and rage. Cap had seen enough to know that Zeke Haynes was a man who ruled his household with voice and fist, while his wife swallowed her anger — until now. Emily glared at her husband's impassive face, her neck bowed with determination to sway him from his righteous single-mindedness.

"Your eldest son," she repeated in a low voice, "is asking for you."

His head slowly turning now, Haynes met her gaze. She repeated her words. After a long moment he lowered the shotgun, turned, and walked through the lighted doorway where the three younger boys stepped aside. The moment he entered the soddy, Emily moved close to Cap.

"Git!"

"Hezekiah didn't speak, did he?"

"Not yet," she said. "But he will. Now, you git!"

Hot summer air bore the smell of rain. Cap rode up the forested ridge behind his cabin, listening to the thunderous growl coming from the black, boiling clouds like the voice of Haynes's vengeful God. After returning to his homestead in the buggy, he had crawled into the brush shelter in the aspen grove and slept until awakened by the thunder. A storm was brewing over the mountains. He had caught his gelding and had headed up the ridge behind his claim.

Now, when he looked back at the charred remains of his cabin, he saw the cook stove amid the ashes and burned logs, stovepipe still slanting to one side. Beyond the corral and water trough, smoke drifted out of a heap of smoldering embers — all that was left of his barn.

From the bench upslope horses whinnied, and the gelding answered. Cap found the draft animals milling there, just as they had after fleeing the grass fire. He rode on and topped the ridge. Water gurgled in the high grass, and, as he forded the brook, he recalled that early morning when he heard the muffled cries of the baby.

Thunder sounded overhead again as Cap picked a route through the darkening forest. Pine boughs slapped at him, so he bent over the horse's neck. The heavy silence before the storm seemed to magnify sounds — the creak of saddle leather, the clink of a bridle chain, a horseshoe ringing against stone — all loud now to his ears.

He was cautious, aware that at any time he might overtake Ashworth and his hired gunmen even though he had lost most of a day by taking Hezekiah to the farm. He examined the horse tracks on the forest floor, all recent, but he could not sort out livery mounts from cavalry horses. Yet, he did not waste precious time in search of tracks. Logic told him Jane and Jamie would first hike to their cache of supplies — either the cave or the lean-to in the camp of Joshua Potter and White Moon Woman — and Ashworth would have reached the same conclusion. But how far would they have traveled since leaving the cabin? And what if Ashworth and his gunmen had already caught up with them?

Cap tried to push these troubling thoughts away. He figured Jane and Jamie as well as Ashworth's group would have stopped sometime in the night to rest. Then at daybreak, he guessed, they would have pressed on to the waterfall and the valley at the base of the mountain. With a strong and rested horse he would have a chance of closing the distance.

He rode into a stand of aspens and halted when the buckskin hopped, ears pinned back. In a small clearing ahead an oval pond reflected the gray light from the sky like tarnished

170

silver. Cap drew rein, one hand clenching the walnut grips of his Colt. He looked around, wondering if a bear or cougar was in the vicinity. Or men.

He dismounted. He saw nothing until distant sounds — soft thumpings — reached his ears. From the aspen grove ahead came the crunching of dried twigs and then a sudden rustle of brush. In the next moment an antlered buck zigzagged through the aspens, running headlong toward him until the horse nickered. Wide-eyed, the buck veered away, gracefully fleeing among the trees to his left. Any number of predators could have spooked the deer, he thought — or human scent. Uneasy, he watched and listened.

A morning breeze whispered through the treetops, bringing fine raindrops. Aspen leaves fluttered. He looked up, realizing he had seen no birds this morning, or any other forest creatures except the deer. The building storm might have silenced them and sent them into hiding.

Cap stayed in the stand of white-barked trees for a time, chewing a piece of salty venison and drinking from his canteen, still listening. Then he eased closer to the pond. The surface of the water was speckled by raindrops. While the horse drank noisily through the bit, he knelt and submerged his canteen. Round, shiny bubbles rushed out of the mouth, the vessel pulsing in his hand like some living creature.

A series of rounded imprints caught his eye. Cap stood, as he corked the canteen. Skirting the pond, he came upon fresh tracks in the mud — six shod horses — and caught the odor of manure before he saw the droppings. Beyond the bank, he examined a patch of bent grass where a trail led into the trees. He quickly returned to his horse and mounted. Riding around the pond, he followed the tracks into the trees, knowing now Ashworth was ahead, but not far ahead.

Rain still sprinkled out of the overcast sky when he reached the crest of the ridge overlooking the waterfall. He descended that steep slope, tracking the livery horses through the lodgepole pines. The distant roar of the waterfall came to him. The tracks led to the creek downstream from the waterfall. At the rocky bank Cap let his horse drink, just as Ashworth's men had stopped here within the last few hours. In the drizzling rain he watched the clear water rush past with mesmerizing speed. The creek rippled over the shiny pebbles and stones — hard, granite-shaped, and smoothed by countless centuries of slow ice and fast water.

This unnamed stream, tumbling out of the Rocky Mountains, eventually joined Trapper Creek in its meandering course across the plains. It flowed into the Platte, the Missouri, and finally into the Mississippi River on its southward run to the Gulf of Mexico. Cap thought about that as he looked around. At higher elevation a glacier melted drop by drop — fresh water frozen in the Ice Age long before mankind trod the earth — and created a headwater rushing for the sea.

He pulled his hat low against the rain and touched spurs to his horse. He rode downstream through the wet pines toward the grassy meadow marked by teepee rings. A sound reached him. He reined up. He heard the whinnies and snorts of horses made restless by the storm. Then a voice uttered a single command, and gunfire erupted from the dark forest ahead.

At the booming reports of repeating rifles, Cap hauled back on the reins and at once reached for his Colt. The gelding sank under him. He leaped free just as the big horse fell and rolled on its side, wheezing its last breaths. Lying prone behind the horse, Cap reached up and yanked his Spencer from the blood-splattered scabbard. He took off his hat and slowly raised up. Peering over the horse, he saw two shadows moving through the black pines, rushing toward him.

He steadied the rifle on the side of the gelding and drew aim. Firing, he quickly levered in a fresh round, aimed, and pulled the trigger again. Both shadows dropped. After a silence he heard sobbing cries. Cap waited several minutes, listening to the pained calls for help. He pulled off his spurs and dropped them into the wet grass. Opening a saddlebag on the exposed side of the horse, he pulled out a box of ammunition and filled his jacket pocket with bullets. He stood and sprinted for the trees.

He angled away from the gunmen, making it to the nearest pine without drawing fire. Moving fast, he made a wide circle. He came up behind two downed gunmen and, on the ground near each man, he saw a new Winchester laying shiny wet. One of the two men was sprawled on the forest floor, eyes open in death. The second gunman lay a dozen yards away amidst a pile of pine needles. Rain-soaked clothes clung to his body and his knees were drawn up to his bloodied chest. He was whimpering. Cap watched the wounded man's eyes squint shut against the pain. He recognized him — Archie.

"You killed my cow horse," he stated as he walked toward the downed man.

The man's eyes opened.

"Mister Ashworth said you'd come," Archie said in a voice barely audible. "Said . . . said we had to kill you . . . or you'd kill us."

"If you hadn't thrown in with him," Cap said, "you'd be headed for home right now. All I ever wanted was for you men to go back to Chicago."

Archie shivered. His eyes closed again.

"Why'd you burn me out?"

Archie answered slowly. "Ashworth . . . promised. . . ."

"Promised what?"

"Me and Leonard," he said, "we can't go back to Chicago

173

. . . law dogs hunting us . . . Ashworth said . . . said he'd build a Reynolds way station on the Cheyenne-Denver road . . . for me and Leonard."

"He's lying to one of us," Cap said.

"What . . . ?"

"He told me Reynolds Overland will be out of business when the U. P. builds a spur to Denver."

Cap saw the man's eyes widen, and knew he had not heard the same story.

"I . . . I ain't going to make it, am I?"

"I'll get you to a doctor as soon as I can."

Cap left him shivering on the wet ground. He moved through the trees, until he reached a gap between two blue spruces. He halted, rifle at the ready. In the meadow that had once been the summer campsite to a band of Cheyennes he saw the livery horses bunched together in the storm. Peering through the drizzling rain, he studied the dense pine forest beyond the meadow.

He figured Ashworth and his men were there somewhere, searching for Potter's lean-to. He wondered what they would do now that they had heard gunshots — would they head back this way?

Turning to his left, he moved swiftly through the trees to the base of the ridge. There he jogged upslope through a patch of open ground to the stand of lodgepole pines. Using the slender trees for cover, he made his way to a high vantage point overlooking the meadow. He knelt, rifle across his legs.

Cap stiffened when he heard the sound of gunfire. The shots had come from the direction of the forest — fifteen or twenty reports from rifles, followed by half a dozen shots from a single weapon. Those last rounds were fired at regular intervals, as a trained cavalryman under attack would return fire.

174

Cap stood, then began descending the slope in downhill leaps between the lodgepoles. Coming out of the trees into the meadow, he ran through the high grass on to the open ground and dashed into the cold dark shadows of the pine forest. Already damp from the rain, the needled branches showered him with water and soaked him from hat brim to boot toes. He lunged ahead. He had to locate Potter's camp in this forest maze, all the time fearing Ashworth and his gunmen had stumbled onto it and had pinned Potter down. He ran on through the pines, slowing his pace when he heard the sound of water gurgling, remembering the hidden creek. He knew he was close.

The water sounds led him to the granite outcropping. He halted when he spotted the lean-to. He saw it because someone had pulled the cut branches away from the structure, exposing it at the bottom of the granite face. Around it, the soft wet ground held the boot tracks of several men.

Cap felt relieved when he found no brass shell casings on the ground and no blood or any other signs of a fight. It was a safe bet that Ashworth had found this camp after a long search, and he had found it empty. From here he probably headed for the cave. The shots must have come from that direction.

So Cap believed, until the low rumble of voices reached his ears. He turned. In the dark forest he glimpsed a number of men rushing through the trees. A moment later shots rang out. At the sound of the repeating rifles, he dove to the ground as the bullets struck the trees around him. Cap rolled. He came up on his elbows and returned the fire, snapping off half a dozen rounds in the direction of the approaching men, and then he quickly rolled to his right. He dug bullets out of his pocket, reloaded, and fired again. He did not expect to hit any of them with his rapid-fire shooting, but he wanted the Ashworth men to know they were in for a fight.

He belly-crawled away, catching another glimpse of four men in the rain darkened forest. Not in a military formation, they formed a hunters' line with each man separated by ten or twelve paces while they advanced, side by side, to flush out their prey.

Cap sent them diving when he fired again, this time spacing half a dozen rounds a few feet apart, waist high. Most of his shots hit trees, but a panicked shout indicated he had hit and wounded at least one of the gunmen. He reloaded, shoving his last bullet into the Spencer.

Chapter Seventeen

Outnumbered, Cap knew he could not allow the gunmen to run him down in this forest. Like his nightmarish memories of war — anticipating a charge by ambushers after his horse was shot out from under him — Cap relived old terrors in those seconds. Unlike the deadly attack on his column in the spring of '65, he had no reason now to stand and fight to save the lives of his men. He got to his feet and ran, dodging through the thick-trunked ponderosas while shoving the wet, overhanging boughs aside with his free hand.

He could hear shouts behind him, and he knew he had been spotted. In the next instant gunshots and the whine of bullets sent him diving to the ground. He slid into a carpet of wet pine needles. Rolling, he sunfished and came up on his elbows, Spencer at the ready. He could not see his attackers from here, but, to slow them down, he fired three quick shots in the direction of their voices.

He came up on his feet and discovered he had lost his revolver. But where, when? He glanced around but could not find the weapon among the pine cones and fallen branches on the forest floor. He knew he could not linger or backtrack, and a feeling of desperation surged through him. Again, he looked left and right. He forced himself to move ahead, catching sight of brass shell casings scattered among the pine needles. He recognized army-issue brass. Potter had to have returned fire from here not that long ago.

Bent low, Cap moved through the trees as fast as he could. Until now he had been guided by his instinct to stretch the distance between himself and Ashworth's group with little thought to direction or destination. One lucky shot from any of them would end the fight, and, as long as the gunmen bore down on him, all odds favored them.

More Spencer shell casings on the ground led toward the mountain slope. Potter had fired his carbine from here. But where had he gone? Was he still alive? Cap guessed Ashworth had either killed Potter or broken off the attack when shots rang out during Cap's brief gunfight with Archie and the other gunman. Ashworth and the others had backtracked until they had spotted Cap among the trees.

Now, with no handgun and five rounds left in the magazine of his rifle, a running gun battle would quickly deplete his ammunition. He remembered the pile of rock débris near the base of the mountain; it afforded cover and long views of the open ground. If he hid among the boulders, he ran the risk of being pinned down, but, at least, he had a chance to defend himself there. He decided to try it.

Cap scanned the thick brush that grew among the granite boulders, now darkened to a gray-black by the rain, a dull color matching the sky. Cap ran toward them. In a bygone era a tremor or the sheer force of gravity had broken the granite outcropping high upslope and sent these boulders crashing down the mountain, exposing the formation of white quartz — and creating the cave.

Thunder rumbled as Cap ran out of the trees and vaulted over a boulder. He nearly landed on a marmot sheltered against the rain. The furry animal let out a single squeak, shook itself, and lumbered away. Cap climbed over the boulder and jumped to another. By climbing and leaping, he made his way upslope out of the brush. He looked back. He had gained a position higher than the tops of the pines in the forest. He quickly looked around. No sign of Potter. His gaze went to a flat-topped boulder half the size of a freight wagon.

Cap moved to it and settled in behind it. Setting his rifle on the flat, wet surface, he confirmed his first impression — this position gave him nearly a full view left to right, down and up, at once offering protection. Lightning flashed overhead. A single firebolt zigzagged from sky to earth. Cap instinctively ducked, even though the lightning had flashed and disappeared in the wink of an eye. He eased up. After looking around, he took stock. In addition to his Colt, he had lost his hat somewhere in the forest. He thought back and remembered drawing the gun when his horse went down. He must have dropped it when he yanked the rifle from the scabbard, and had probably lost his hat there, too. Sweeping a hand over his brow, he pushed the wet hair back from his forehead.

Minutes passed. He heard a sound. Leaning forward, he looked down. In the rocks below, surprisingly close, a tall, black-bearded man was climbing toward him, Winchester in hand.

Cap grabbed his Spencer. The sound of the barrel scraping across stone drew the man's attention. When he saw Cap, he swiftly brought the rifle to his shoulder and snapped off a shot. His aim went wild. At nearly the same moment Cap raised his Spencer. He fired, knowing at once he had missed. He levered another round into the chamber and lined up the sights, while the black-bearded man did the same. This time Cap was a split-second faster when he pulled the trigger.

The bullet caught the gunman squarely in the chest. The force of it knocked him back and sent his wet hat tumbling off his head as though blown by a gust of wind. The Winchester fell from his grasp and clattered against the rocks. Cap stared at the dead man sprawled over a boulder, one booted foot sticking up, when a second rifle boomed. He ducked. The shot came from his right and ricocheted off a rock behind him.

He heard a shout. Another man answered. He listened, but heard only his pounding heartbeat and the dull roar in his ears from his own shooting. The gunmen were probably on the move. Waiting for them to improve their positions would be suicidal. He had to prevent the men from closing in — somehow. Cap eased up behind the flat stone surface. The moment he presented a target, more shots rang out. Bullets whined off the stone all around him.

"McKenna!"

Cap recognized Ashworth's voice.

"Come out! We'll talk!"

Moving as far as possible to his left, Cap checked the Spencer. He drew a deep breath and exhaled. Raindrops ran down his face. Ashworth called his name again.

"McKenna! I assure you, I want no fight with you. Throw down your guns. Walk out peaceably."

In response Cap counted to ten and then quickly sprang up on his knees. Aiming at the lone gunman downslope to his right, he fired. Then, swiveling in the direction of Ashworth's voice, he worked the lever and fired again. Just as he dropped behind the boulder, six shots answered his two. He now knew the approximate locations of the gunmen, and he realized they had climbed higher in the rocks. They were closing in, but with one of them dead, he hoped he had given those remaining a reason to think twice before charging his position.

Cap remembered the Winchester dropped by the dead man and wished he had a way to retrieve it. If he could hold out until dark. . . . No sooner had the thought entered his mind, than he dismissed it, certain that Ashworth would not let a stalemate go on that long. His gunmen would tighten the noose before nightfall, or die trying.

Cap raised up again, slowly this time, and just far enough to see the jumble of boulders below — and again more shots

180

rang out. He ducked down. The back of his neck stung. He reached back. His fingertips felt blood from several tiny cuts. Bullet fragments or stone shards must have hit him.

He was absently watching as the fine rain washed the blood from his fingers, when thunder cracked sharply overhead. He looked up just as the sky was suddenly illuminated by a bolt of lightning. It flashed and struck with a loud bang. He nudged himself up in time to see the crown of a pine tree sputtering fire and smoke like a huge torch. A flame in this rain seemed impossible, and Cap was momentarily captivated by the phenomenon.

Then thunder crackled again, louder this time, so sudden and close that it felt as though the explosion was next to his ear. Blinding light flashed out of the black sky once, twice, and a third time, filling the air with an acrid smell. With the storm's cannonade came a strange sight. Transfixed, Cap stared at a large ball of lightning as it appeared to roll across the surface of the rockslide, a swift oval of bright fire spinning over the jagged, wet boulders. It disappeared as quickly as it had struck. Cap had heard of ball lightning, but had never seen it — and would not have believed it, if he had not seen it for himself.

He realized this was his chance and raised himself up higher behind the boulder. No shots were fired by the gunmen. Either they had been stunned by the lightning, or as dazzled as he had been in that moment when time seemed frozen by fire. Cap grabbed his Spencer and climbed out from behind the boulder. He was met by silence.

Turning, he climbed upward, leaping from the flat-topped boulder to the one above, and up to the next. He climbed until he heard rifle shots, the bullets zinging past him like bees stirred from a hive. Cap ducked and tried to find cover. None of the boulders here gave him complete protection. He glanced back and saw Ashworth and the two gunmen, one of them Leonard, coming for him, pausing as they climbed to aim and shoot at him.

Then rifle reports sounded from higher up on the mountainside. The shots were evenly timed. At first he thought one of the men had gained a new position, and he was doomed. But then he heard shouts of alarm from Ashworth's men. Those gunshots had come from someone else — Potter!

Cap looked down the rockslide. Amid the din of three Winchesters firing rapidly there, he saw one of the men aiming his repeater upward, almost as though pointing at the stormy sky. Cap figured the man had Potter in his sights. He drew aim and squeezed the trigger, the butt plate slamming against his shoulder. The man pitched suddenly to one side, his rifle falling from his hands.

More shots came from high on the mountainside. Cap looked up and saw muzzle flashes from the black cave — red flame, darting like a snake's tongue. Cap could not see Potter, but he recognized the report from a Spencer repeater. He turned. Down below, Leonard was not deterred. He darted from one rain-wet boulder to another, as he closed in.

Cap quickly worked the lever. He brought his Spencer to his shoulder and lined up the sights. Squeezing the trigger, he heard a click. Leonard had advanced close enough to hear it, too, and called out to the other man. Both fired a volley to drive Potter into the cave. Then Leonard began to ascend again, rifle in hand as he moved in for the kill. A moment later one shot from the cave split his head open and sent him tumbling, head over heels, slamming against the rocks as he crashed down. The other man tried to flee, but no sooner had he left his position than he was dropped by a single shot from Potter's carbine.

"Cap!"

Looking up the steep slope of the rockslide, he saw the big man standing on a boulder at the mouth of the cave.

"Cap, he's running! Ashworth's running!"

Cap looked down the slide and caught sight of a shadow moving swiftly in the brush. Standing, he leaped to the boulder directly below him, and then leaped again. He continued to jump from one boulder to another, driven by the knowledge that he had to head Ashworth off before he reached the horses.

Just as he was gaining speed, Cap's foot slipped, his boot sliding off the flat surface of a rain-slick boulder. The rock shifted. Pain shot through his ankle as the boulder fell against the next one like a trap snapping shut. Cap pulled. His foot was held fast between the two boulders. He leaned back and pulled again. The more he strained to free himself, the tighter the rocks seemed to hold. He twisted, grimacing, and tried to yank his leg out at a different angle, but the boot was jammed. It would not budge.

Breathing hard from the exertion, Cap heard a deep voice from above. He looked upslope and saw Potter rushing down the rockslide toward him, followed by Jane and Jamie. Beyond them, White Moon Woman appeared at the mouth of the cave. She stayed there, holding the blanket-wrapped baby in her arms.

"What happened?" Potter asked before he saw Cap's foot wedged in between the rocks.

Assessing the situation, he moved below Cap, studying the granite boulders. Both were large, weighing several hundred pounds each. Potter grabbed the top of one boulder with both hands. He tried lifting and shoving, in an attempt to dislodge it. And, as he lifted, Cap pulled back. Neither the boulder nor his foot would budge. Potter changed positions. He tried to move the other boulder — without success.

"Go on," Cap said. "Go after Ashworth."

Potter shook his head, his skin shining with rain and sweat. "Not until I get you out of this fix."

Jane and Jamie finally reached them. Together with Potter, they tried to rock the boulders from side to side, first one, then the other, while Cap tried to slide his foot out in spite of the severe pain caused by even attempting to move it.

"Oh, Cap," Jane whispered in anguish, "what are we going to do?"

"Go after Ashworth," Cap said again. "Stop him!"

When Potter answered with one shake of his head, Cap looked around. His gaze went to his rifle. He leaned over as far as he could and picked up the Spencer. "Use this for a pry bar," he said.

Potter took the gun and jammed the barrel down between the two boulders. He grasped the stock and with all of his weight behind it, he pried.

Cap felt a twinge. The boulder moved slightly, but not enough.

Potter tried again, this time with Jane's help. The boulder moved, but the rifle barrel bent. Cap felt the heavy granite shift back to rest on his ankle.

"Try both of them," Cap said, motioning to Potter's gun.

Potter put the carbine and rifle side by side and inserted the barrels into the gap between the boulders. Grasping the stocks, he pried again, grunting. Jane moved to his side and pushed against them, too.

Cap felt the pressure relieved from his ankle. "Harder."

With renewed effort, Potter shoved again, muscles bulging, face contorted. Jane shoved, too. This time the boulder moved half an inch.

Cap pulled the foot free. He rolled clear of the boulder and sat up.

"Do you think you'll be able to walk?" Potter asked.

Cap felt a surge of pain when he touched his ankle. But his foot moved freely. With Potter's help, he stood and gingerly put weight on it.

"Nothing broken," he replied, "just some pain when I. . . ."

Jane interrupted: "Where's Jamie?"

Cap looked around, surprised to discover the boy was nowhere in sight. "He was right here a few minutes ago. Wasn't he?"

"Maybe he hiked back to the cave," Potter suggested, looking upslope.

Jane called his name. When no answer came, she called again, louder.

The three of them stood there, bewildered by his disappearance. Jane started climbing up the rockslide toward the cave, but halted when two shots rang out from the forest below.

She whirled around, a look of panic flooding her face. "He went after Mister Ashworth!"

Cap nearly fell over as Potter released him, drew his handgun, and started down the rockslide. Gaining his balance, he followed, limping and wincing each time he put his weight on the foot that had been trapped. Jane passed him by as she raced down the slide. He saw her leap recklessly from one boulder to another and doubted she would make it to the bottom without falling.

But she did. He watched her overtake Potter and lost sight of both of them when they ran into the trees. Cap cursed as he made the slow decent, favoring his right ankle, until at last he reached the base of the rockslide. Then he limped to the wet forest. Through a break in the trees ahead he saw the saddle horses, grazing peacefully. Fording the creek, he came into the meadow.

Potter had holstered his revolver. Jane stood at Jamie's side, her arm around his shoulders. The youth held a Winchester trained on Stanley Ashworth.

"Don't worry, Cap!" Jamie called out when he saw him. "I've got him! He's not going anywhere!"

Cap joined them, listening to Jamie's account of his quick action. The boy had taken Cap's suggestion to Potter to heart and took it upon himself to detain Ashworth. Jamie had grabbed a Winchester dropped by one of the gunmen. Rushing into the meadow, he had gotten the drop on Ashworth. When the man had challenged him, Jamie had fired two shots at Ashworth's feet and then disarmed him.

"Nothing to it Cap," Jamie said proudly.

The rain ceased in the afternoon, but gray, misty clouds hung over the treetops like a shroud. Their clothes wet, they all shivered in the meadow, until White Moon Woman joined them. Jane held the baby while White Moon Woman sparked flint into dry wood chips from her camp and built a fire.

After they had warmed themselves and tied up Ashworth, Cap went in search of Archie. He found him near the other dead gunman, lying on a carpet of pine needles, knees drawn to his chest in death. Potter had accompanied him to the site of the two dead men.

The big man glanced skyward. "A proper day for buryin'," he said.

He brought a trenching tool from his camp, and the two of them dug graves in dark wet earth near the sloping stand of lodgepole pines. Cap's ankle pained him, so Potter did most of the work. Similarly, they dug graves near the rockslide. When they had finished, five men lay in their final resting places, in unmarked graves.

All this time Jamie guarded Ashworth at gunpoint. Cap

overheard the man alternately making threats and lavish promises to Jane in his efforts to gain his freedom. None of his words mattered until dusk, when the saddle horses whinnied and unseen horses answered. Moments later troopers appeared, weapons at the ready. The dozen men were led by Major Luke Symington.

Symington swept into the camp at a canter, his troopers swiftly encircling Potter, White Moon Woman, Jane and Jamie, and Ashworth. Cap noticed Marcus was among them. The trooper's face showed alarm, and Cap realized he was looking at Jamie. Quickly turning, Cap motioned for the boy to lower the Winchester. The youth grudgingly complied.

Ashworth immediately addressed Symington, who remained on his mount, surveying the situation. "Major, I am grateful for your rescue! These . . . these outlaws confined me. They murdered men in my employ. . . ."

Jamie jumped forward and shouted: "He's lying! He's lying!"

Symington dismounted. He listened for several minutes to the myriad accusations being shouted by Jane and Jamie, each one countered by Ashworth. Then he lifted a hand for silence.

"Major," Ashworth said, "I shall make a report to your superior officer. . . ."

Symington turned to him. "You'll have your day in court to prove your innocence."

"What the devil are you talking about?"

"On my way here, Mister Ashworth, I interviewed a young fellow by the name of Hezekiah Haynes."

Cap stepped closer. "Is he all right, then?"

Symington glanced at him and nodded. "On the mend, and eager to tell me about Ashworth and his hired gunmen."

"Sir, I have never heard of the gentleman," Ashworth said.

"You shot him and left him for dead," Symington said,

turning to face him, "when you set fire to McKenna's homestead."

Flustered, Ashworth said: "You will take the word of someone I've never even laid eyes on. . . ."

"He tried to kill us!" Jamie interrupted.

"I merely defended myself. . . ."

Symington again lifted a hand for quiet. "At dawn I will escort you to Denver . . . all of you. That's all I have to say."

Despite protests, Ashworth was placed under guard. The troopers made camp in the meadow and built a fire from the coals of White Moon Woman's campfire.

The rain clouds broke, the sky cleared, and the wet grass reflected the starlight like fresh paint. Marcus and the other troopers gathered around Potter, smoking and talking as he knelt at their fire.

Symington took Cap aside. He held his hand out to shake. "Sorry we came to blows, McKenna."

Cap grasped his hand.

"If anything good came of that beating you handed me," he went on, "it gave me authority to ride after you with a squad of men." He paused. "After I left the Haynes farm, I knew Tom had landed on the wrong side of this thing. You were right about Ashworth. I'll inform the colonel. No criminal charges will be lodged against you."

"You're sure?" Cap asked doubtfully.

Symington nodded. "Tom is leaving his command."

"Leaving," Cap repeated.

"He requires more medical treatment for his wound than our sawbones can provide," Symington said. "That was a war arrow that hit him . . . the edges chipped to leave sharp barbs. A surgeon will have to cut deep to remove it. A new commanding officer will be dispatched to Denver within thirty days. In the interim, I will command the Ninth."

At dawn Cap made a discovery, after he had pulled on his boots with some discomfort. Walking the perimeter of the meadow, he confirmed it — Potter and White Moon Woman had slipped away in the night.

As Cap returned to the center of the camp, he heard Ashworth state to Symington — "Negligence of duty, Major." Since a prisoner of the United States Army had escaped, the lawyer offered to "keep this between gentlemen." In return, he would leave Denver on the first coach. He watched Symington respond with a shake of his head. Ashworth grew agitated and grasped at Symington's sleeve. The major pulled free and threatened to place him in irons.

"Potter's the one who should have been shackled!" Ashworth said loudly. "I will report his escape to Colonel Sully."

"Escape?" Symington said deadpan. "Who escaped?"

Ashworth stared at him.

"No one has seen Potter," Symington said.

"Major, are you insane?"

He turned to his troopers. "Have any of you men seen Sergeant Joshua Potter?"

Cap surveyed the puzzled looks. The troopers glanced at one another. Marcus grinned. When he laughed aloud, smiles crept over the faces of the troopers.

"No, suh, Major," Marcus said. "We haven't seen ol' Josh Potter."

"No, suh!" echoed another.

The words — "We ain't seen him!" — passed through the lips of every trooper present.

Ashworth shouted: "I'll have you court-martialed . . . every damned one of you!"

Chapter Eighteen

"Cap, oh, Cap," Jane whispered, her voice on the verge of breaking.

He heard her distraught voice. Along with Jamie, Cap and Jane brought up the rear, and had just ridden out of the trees on the ridge overlooking the homestead. The squad of blue-clad men stretched out ahead with Stanley Ashworth flanked by a pair of troopers.

"Cap, I'm so sorry," she said, turning in the saddle.

Jamie, too, stared at the burned ruins of the cabin and barn.

Cap's attention was drawn to a freight wagon amidst the charred remains of his homestead. The rig stood near the aspen grove. He took it all in — the corral was still intact, along with the undamaged water trough, and there stood the Reynolds horses, confined, facing the approaching riders as though expecting their ration of oats. Then, out of the eerie silence, Cap heard a familiar voice.

The party on the ridge top listened to complaints about the hardships of working as a freighter, laced with a healthy dose of cursing, by a diminutive figure who was striding out of the shade of the aspens.

Cap smiled when he recognized Dud Dawkins who wore his usual black vest over a red flannel shirt.

In the lead, Symington approached the teamster, who yanked off his battered hat and spat in disgust.

"Major, 'bout damned time you and your army got here! Some yokel burned Cap out! Look at this! You see this? Catch the bastard who done set this fire. Catch him and hang him!"

Cap spurred his livery horse ahead. When Dud saw him, he waved his hat. Mad as a wet bantam rooster, he listened impatiently as Cap told him what had happened.

"Well, let's hang that son-of-a-bitch from the tallest tree!" he shouted.

Symington answered tersely, informing Dud the accused man would stand before a federal judge in court. He turned his horse and rode on to Trapper Creek with Dud muttering after him.

Jane and Jamie caught up while Cap thanked Dud for gathering the horses. "You saved those plugs from becoming cougar and bear food."

"I missed one jughead," Dud replied. "A bay mare ran off, hell for leather."

"Figures," Cap said.

Dud went on: "I had just hitched up a fresh team and was fixing to pull out when I seen them troopers come off the ridge." He drew a deep breath and looked around helplessly. "Still say they oughta just hang the bastard and be done with it. Damn, Cap. What're you gonna do?"

A woman's voice answered: "Rebuild."

Cap turned and saw that Jane had ridden close to them.

"Cap will rebuild," she repeated. "Reynolds Overland will pay for the construction of a new barn and cabin . . . and everything else Cap lost."

Cap introduced Jane and Jamie to the teamster, explaining to the sister and brother that they had this man to thank for rounding up the draft horses.

"You have my gratitude," Jane said. "A bonus will be in your next pay envelope."

"I don't care about that," Dud said bluntly. "I gotta to know what's gonna happen."

"Sir?" Jane said.

Dud shaded his eyes with his hat as he looked up at Jane, who remained on horseback. "Yes, ma'am. I gotta know. Is Reynolds Overland rolling, or ain't it?"

She smiled. "As long as men like you are willing to haul freight, Mister Dawkins, Reynolds Overland will stay on the road." She smiled and then added: "The job that needs to be done right now is to haul oats and supplies here, to Cap's homestead. Can you make a run to Denver and back?"

Dud turned his head and spat a stream of brown tobacco juice. "Yes, ma'am! I'm halfway there and back."

After Dawkins had left, Jane confided to Cap: "I don't know if Reynolds Overland can compete with the Union Pacific. The company may fail. All I know is. . . ."

"Daddy would want us to try!" Jamie broke in with a loud laugh to finish her thought.

Jane smiled at her brother.

The column stopped for water at the Haynes farm. Cap saw the door of the soddy swing open. Emily Haynes stepped into the bright sunlight with Hezekiah behind her, barefooted and hatless. The youth halted when he saw Ashworth.

Cap dismounted and hurried to him with Jane and Jamie following. Hezekiah's head was wrapped with a bandage fashioned from a flour sack. His frowning gaze swept past Ashworth, and he grinned when he saw Cap.

"Good to see you on your feet," Cap said, meeting him on the footpath between the rows of flowering hollyhocks.

"Yes, sir, Cap. In a few days I'll be ready to come back to work for you. We've got livestock to tend, a cabin to build. . . ."

Emily reached out and put her hand on his shoulder. "He'll stay here until he's healed."

Hezekiah grinned when Cap advised him to heed his mother.

"The job will be waiting for you . . . ," Cap began.

"I captured the man who shot you, Hezekiah!" Jamie broke in. "I got a Winchester off a dead man, and I fired two shots!"

Cap explained that Stanley Ashworth was in custody and recounted the events since the night Hezekiah had been shot. As he finished, Symington joined them.

"That 'ere man, he's the one who shot me," Hezekiah said, pointing to Ashworth. "He shot me and then he done burned Cap out."

Symington nodded. "I need a written statement from you. Will you co-operate fully in the investigation?"

"Yes, sir," Hezekiah said, "I sure will."

After the major returned to his horse and rode to the water trough, Emily stepped closer to Cap. "Zeke, he's out in the field with the boys. Good thing he ain't here. He reckons you're Satan's agent. You turned son against father, my Zeke says. He's a-scared the other boys will take a notion to run off, too." She paused, the wrinkles deepening in her face as her jaw clenched. "I done told him Hezekiah's near growed up. Best let him work nearby, instead of running off to the gold fields. Zeke, he blames you fer putting such thoughts in my head."

"You lied to me, McKenna . . . more than once. Now, after you and Major Symington beat the hell out of each other, you've got him lying to me, too."

Cap stood before Tom Sully in the lobby of the Denver House. Symington had sent him there from the headquarters tent at the Platte encampment after taking a statement detailing his knowledge of the crimes committed by Stanley Ashworth. Before Cap departed, the major had confided that Sully's career in the Army hung in the balance now. If he failed to regain complete use of his arm after surgery, he would be forced to retire with the rank of colonel, his dream of attaining general dashed.

Now in full uniform with his right arm in a sling, Sully sat in a wicker chair by the front window. He had been moved here from the field camp for his comfort. An ambulance wagon would carry him to Cheyenne with four troopers guarding Ashworth, and there they would board the eastbound train.

"The major has presented me with overwhelming evidence of Ashworth's guilt," Sully went on, "and I will personally escort that man to Chicago as a prisoner of the United States Army."

Cap saw the man grimace when he shifted his weight in the cushioned armchair.

"Don't get puffed up, McKenna," he said. "I concede you were right about Ashworth, but you'll hear no apology from me. Fact is, you should be begging my forgiveness."

Cap looked at him curiously.

"You knew of the attack on my column, and you could have warned me. But you were intent on executing your plan for Potter's escape. Now, that's the truth, isn't it?"

"No, sir."

Sully scowled. "I do not believe for a moment one Indian woman routed my entire command and turned Potter loose single-handedly. I do not believe that, any more than I believe Symington failed to locate Sergeant Joshua Potter in those mountains. Not for one damned moment do I believe those lies." He drew a breath. "If I were able, I'd go after Potter myself. And I'd bring him in, shackled. You may be certain of that."

When Cap made no reply, Sully commanded: "Look me in the eye, mister. Look me in the eye, and tell me you had no hand in the attack on my column."

194

"I told you once," Cap said evenly. "I don't aim to tell you again."

"You, sir, are a liar."

Cap met his gaze in silence.

"Not even man enough to speak in your own defense, are you, McKenna? Worse than a common liar, you are a coward. Get out of my sight."

An awkward moment came after the last handshake with Jamie and a parting embrace with Jane. Good byes were said and promises made to meet again. With a shout and pop of the whip over the team of six, the red Concord stagecoach lurched away. Cap stepped back from a cloud of rising dust, his mind churning with memories of all that had happened since the day he had first shaken hands with J. Stuart Reynolds.

Several minutes later his reverie was broken when the coach returned, headed for the livery. The driver called out, reporting one of the horses had pulled up lame and would have to be replaced. When the stagecoach came to a rocking halt, Jane and Jamie climbed out with the other passengers. Limping slightly, Cap joined them on the boardwalk under an awning. Having parted once, none of them spoke for several uncomfortable minutes. Jamie drifted away to watch the livery man change the horses under the close scrutiny of the driver. Jane looked around, her gaze moving to the distant mountains. The highest peaks were topped with snow under the bright sun of morning.

"Life out here," she mused, "is so different than anything I ever experienced in the city." After a pause she added: "I've been thinking about . . . about everything . . . all I've learned from you and from White Moon Woman. I owe you more than I can ever repay. I feel so bad . . . you lost everything . . . because of me. . . ."

"Because of Ashworth," he corrected.

Eyes blinking, she reflected: "I still think of Daddy. I remember his voice as he read to me and talked to me. More than ever, I believe the words of the visionary essayist. . . . 'out here in the West I am reborn.' "

In a strange way, Cap thought, he was, too. He had slept long and hard in a real bed in the Denver House and awakened refreshed. His shirt and trousers, just yesterday off the dry goods shelf, were stiff. His new hat did not sit comfortably on his head, the brim unfamiliar when he reached up to tug it into place. Shaved and bathed, he was clean and combed now, and bore the scent of cologne from Dave's barbershop. But there was something more, something else different.

"Jamie and I will come back," she said again. "We'll climb another mountain. We'll sleep under the Western stars by night and explore the great forests by day."

With a fresh horse in collar, the driver announced the stagecoach was ready to roll. Once again Cap helped Jane inside. After another good bye and handshake with Jamie, he stepped back, and the high-wheeled vehicle pulled away.

It was true that he had lost nearly everything he owned, every valued possession from his war medals to his cow horse. Yet, instead of a sense of loss, he felt at peace now. At peace. The agony of war had left him. Ghosts of dead soldiers no longer marched through his dreams. No more did he awaken to the screams of young men dying.

Cap remembered the loneliness that washed over him after White Moon Woman left his homestead. The cries of the baby had awakened a yearning. And now he knew. He knew he could rebuild his cabin and barn, tend his stock, and carve his ranch out of the wilderness. More than that, he knew the one thing he could not do. He could not build a home without a family.

Crossing the rutted street from the livery, he stepped up on the boardwalk at the Rocky Mountain Café. He thought of Anna's smile and lingering gaze, and wondered if she had been thinking about him, too. His boots sounding unevenly on the planks of the boardwalk because of his limp, he pulled open the café door, knowing he would soon find out.

About the Author

Stephen Overholser was born in Bend, Oregon, the middle son of Western author, Wayne D. Overholser. Convinced, in his words, that "there was more to learn outside of school than inside," he left Colorado State College in his senior year. He was drafted and served in the U. S. Army in Vietnam. Following his discharge, he launched his career as a writer, publishing three short stories in *Zane Grey Western Magazine*. On a research visit to the University of Wyoming at Laramie, he came across an account of a shocking incident that preceded the Johnson County War in Wyoming in 1892. It was this incident that became the inspiration for his first novel, A HANGING AT SWEETWATER (1974), that received the Spur Award from the Western Writers of America. MOLLY AND THE CONFIDENCE MAN (1975) followed, the first in a series of books about Molly Owens, a clever, resourceful, and tough undercover operative working for a fictional detective agency in the Old West. Among the most notable of Stephen Overholser's later titles are SEARCH FOR THE FOX (1976) and TRACK OF A KILLER (1982). The author is currently at work on his next Five Star Western.